Spit Toon's Saloon

Rinnce and Spit Toon, Proprietors

Sad Songs and Funny Tales on Tap

by

Eric Kobb Miller

WingSpan Press

Printed in the United States of America
Published by WingSpan Press, Livermore, CA
www.wingspanpress.com
The WingSpan name, logo and colophon are the trademarks of WingSpan Publishing.

First Edition 2010
ISBN 978-1-59594-384-2
Library of Congress Control Number: 2010927361

For

Rinnce, Spittella, Brian-Brian, "Nuclear," and "Energy"

THE FAMILY TOON

In a matter of seconds in a previous century, an immigration officer at Ellis Island shortened the family name of my grandfather from Tonacchio to Toon — and *voilà* — I lost a part of me before I was me. And that is why I have always believed that I have been dancing to a different tune all of my life.

To me, Toon does not sound quite as lyrical as Tonacchio. The *oon* sound seems to emit a hint of a whine or a groan. This may all be due, in part or entirety, to my tin ear. But whatever the reason, I have lived my life on a taut trampoline of bouncing memories from which I catch the melodies in the symphonic fugue of the family Toon. I call these melodies "Spit tunes," and I try to orchestrate them into my life.

So, if you're willing to give my Spit tunes a listen, maybe you and your partner can take a few turns on the dance floor here at Spit Toon's Saloon.

CALL ME SPIT

Call me Spit; everyone does, except my mother who still calls me Salvatore. I like to think of myself as a big, bright picture kind of guy, but as Salvatore Spittell Toon, D.M.D., my daily view of life is the small, dark, wet, malodorous, confined space of oral cavities. It's no surprise; it's what a dentist sees, smells, and feels.

Now, don't get me wrong, dentistry is a noble profession, but it requires a lot of swimming upstream in saliva. So, while I wait for local anesthesia to take, an impression to set, a filling to harden, or a dental cement to dry; my mind wanders in search of a way out of the mouth and into the world. I hear my inner voice crying out in verse: "Every day I look at teeth, and teeth stare back at me. Every day I wonder, as I stare out at some tree, if molars could think like dentists, and incisors' minds roam free, would they also pause and ponder what else they'd like to be?"

Caught in crosscurrents of daydreaming and night sweats, the serpentine pathways of my mind take me to a special place. Located in a nondescript neighborhood on the other side of town, it gives no signs of warmth or welcome. Peeling paint creates the illusion of a pockmarked exterior, and the unlit neon sign in the window pushes you away, rather than drawing you in. It is the kind of place you discover serendipitously, stumble upon, or happen to be in front of when a sudden deluge of rain forces you through the door. It was on just such a night that I found myself looking through that window and then placing my hand on the doorknob that led me into Spit Toon's Saloon.

The saloon is a playground where things are brighter, dryer, more open, and more fun; unencumbered by face masks, face shields, goggles, rubber gloves, and surgical gowns. It is here that I recreate the past, embellish the present, and dream the future; changing names, not to protect the innocent, but to entertain myself with sad songs and funny tales.

It is a place for storytelling. Like jigsaw puzzle pieces, stories and poems come individually, incomplete, and in varied shapes, sizes, and colors. They are like whiskey shots and beer chasers, but they do not follow any particular sequence. Instead, they come unannounced at their own time and pace. The flashing pointillistic images begin to connect, one at a time, and then in clusters that coalesce. A life appears revealing its span and depth. Like wine bottles on a rack, or whiskey bottles on a bar, the separate images fight to be seen and to stand out in the crowd. Each bottle holds a memory waiting to be remembered, a dream waiting to be lived, and a life waiting to be told. What was real is forgotten, the facts change, and the stories mix together in a stream of fanciful consciousness. Life becomes fusion fiction. My life is lived in the groove of my own bullspit.

DREAM

Delicious, capricious, and surreptitious;
tinted and printed with a Muse's cues,
a dream slipped over me and settled within.

Lightly and joyously the dalliance played
as a scattered, overturned potpourri of jigsaw
edges lustfully clasped in a clenching embrace.

But when I awoke, my tableau was an empty,
forgotten feeling of blue: a wasteland filled
with the regret of a dalliance denied.

SCRUMPTIOUS

A woodpile of meaningless words
was toppled by a poet's pen, then
placed in a scrum where, with
outstretched arms wrapped around
one another's broad, aching
shoulders, they wallowed in the mud
of battle until they licked the
scrumptious taste of victory which
was as sweet as a poem.

FLASHING

For as long as I can remember, I have always wanted to write "the great American novel" and to be inducted into the pantheon of American writers alongside Melville, Twain, Fitzgerald, Hemingway, and Salinger. An invitation to the literary pantheon not forthcoming, I battled with the demons of low self-esteem. My wife Rinnce, my dental assistant Saliva Godiva, and my dental hygienist Bidday O'Shea all suggested that I try my hand at "flashing." I recoiled in revulsion at the thought of running stark naked through life, in very public places, flashing very private parts. They assured me that the flashing to which they referred was writing very short, short stories which could be entered in writing contests. Doing this would get me focused, disciplined, tournament tough, and hopefully published someday.

Alas, the acceptance letters never came, although the rejection slips inundated my mailbox. It disappointed me, to be sure, but the comments about my punctuation just outright enraged me. Editors constantly criticized how I used my colon, as if that were any of their concern. Moreover, they claimed that my semicolons were acting like squatters in places they didn't belong. As for my commas, they described them as looking like insects randomly stuck between the teeth of a motorcyclist without a face shield — even going so far as to label me a "comma splicer."

One especially unhappy editor, who thought she was Portia in *The Merchant of Venice*, told me that my quotation marks "droppeth not as the gentle rain from heaven upon the place beneath, but as sleet wrapped irritatingly around the wrong words." My penchant for not italicizing the French words I liked to sprinkle about in my text really drove some editors crazy, especially because I italicized my poems which were in English. But more than anything, the endless discussions about hyphens, en dashes, and em dashes felt like acupuncture with dull needles. To this day, I still try to crawl into the spaces which are not supposed to be surrounding my em dashes.

However, I kept tap, tap, tapping away at my keyboard to get even in my own personal and special way. Each time my middle finger, that ubiquitous devil, was to hit a key, I did it with just a tad more emphasis: a flourish which never failed to give me the faintest hint of a smile, even though it inserted more colons: semicolons; commas, and "quotation marks" in all the wrong places, as well as the wrong sized dashes – with inappropriate spaces — between the wrong words.

AT THE END OF MY ROPE

The sun was a spinning
wheel spitting out threads
of heat which wrapped
themselves around my neck
and chest, squeezing sweat
from my spongy skin.
Walls of heat sucked
space away, leaving me
captive in a cell of
claustrophobia.
Fast moving traffic crossing
the bridge pushed me closer to
the edge of terror, where
a reflection from the
surface of the black water
below beckoned to me with
the devilish cackle of death.
Spent by the endless agonizing over
what I was prepared to do, I looked
to the heavens seeking forgiveness.
With my arms extended, leaning
against a suspension wire, the shadow
of a man lashed to a cross blackened
the cloudless sky.
I plummeted headfirst to the devilish
heat below, glaring into the dark
water I was about to enter,
but just as Death reached up to take
me, the bungee cord pulled me back
and lifted me to another jump.

ERGONOMICALLY SPEAKING

Writing is not without its physical perils. Tap, tap, tapping away, hunched over a keyboard, takes its toll on the body. It is not uncommon on a Monday morning for a writer to be confused with a football player, as the writer is stiff, contorted, hobbling, and in pain. Such was my dilemma as I played the wistful knight-errant in quest of the great American novel. My body was in a state of infinite, exponential spasm from my scalp to the soles of my feet. I was so cramped that I finally camped out at the office of Touchy McFeeley, a massage therapist. Touchy was a big proponent of ergonomics, the science of properly positioning a worker to the demands of his job to prevent body strain and injury.

"Unravel those pretzel-like contortions with the music of ergonomics," Touchy prescribed with a lyrical lilt.

"Yeah, yeah," I moaned. "I know that song you're singing, but you know that I can't carry a tune. I guess I need ergonomic singing lessons. Do you know an instructor who can help me?"

"Indeed, I do," Touchy said, beaming. "You should see Lido Libido, a musical therapist whose torch song style is so hot that you'll never have muscle stiffness again."

I found Lido's personality to be magnetic. A name like Lido Libido has a way of creating that effect. Lido performed miracles on my body, doing a flamenco dance on my back in flaming, stiletto high heels while singing "Hey Spit, you've got your chair's too low and your arms are too short, occupational safety and health, you don't fit into your workplace, ergonomic blues. What you need to be singing is I'm not going to you Baby; come to me."

I knew that Touchy had picked the right therapist. What Lido did with high heeled heat fit the bill, and now, so do I.

PITCH

Percussive marital meanderings
led my wife and me inharmoniously
to a musical therapist, who diagnosed
our situation as polyphony.
"You interact within a contrapuntal
fugue, rather than in concert, as two
independent melodic lines, each in
counterpoint to the other," she sang
in coloratura that was as displeasing
to my eyes as to my ears.
"The key to a harmonious marriage is
striking the chord of accord," she harped,
over and over again to the beat of a
metronome.
She noted that my voice had the sound
of a lyre, to which I took offense, but
her pitch was a hanging curve, and I
used a bow to stroke a note with the sound
of a home run, which was where we went
and how we got there.

COUCHING MY WORDS

The rising pile of rejected stories wore away at my self-esteem and confidence. I knew it was time to put myself in the chair of my therapist to, once and for all, put a net over the butterfly of confidence that continued to elude me. Yes, the chair. You see, my therapist, Dr. Lyon Couch, lies on the couch, but not untruthfully, with his pacifier hanging from a chain around his neck, while his patient sits in a chair. Who am I to judge? Some dentists sit; some dentists stand. As the French say: *Chacun à son goût*, which means something like "Use your own pacifier!" Lyon, ever the hail-fellow-well-met, greeted me with a smiling face which turned on a dime to his professional visage upon lying down.

"Spit, how many times have we talked about your awful metaphors? Come down from the clouds and stand in the mud with the rest of us," my therapist said.

"Oh, if they're as bad as yours, I guess you're right," I mumbled.

"Listen," Lyon continued, "I know that you want to write the great American novel and to match your butterfly with Melville's whale, but whatever you write is commendable on its own terms."

"As a flash fiction writer of very short, short stories? Get real, Doc," I said, mockingly.

"Woof, woof," Lyon barked back. "You know that it's the size of the bark, not the size of the dog, that counts. Lincoln's *Gettysburg Address*; Churchill's *Blood, Sweat, and Tears* speech; and Sojourner Truth's *Ain't I a Woman?* speech are each only a few hundred words in length. In fiction there can be truth, and in truth there can be fiction. Those speeches are short, like flash fiction, with a framed message that can capture a feeling, a sense of time, and inspire beyond dry, indisputable fact with a poetic touch."

"You're a real piece of work, Lyon, but thanks for the nice try," I replied.

"Remember, Spit, you're a runner. People run the distance with which they're most comfortable and effective. Keep on writing, one word at a time. Run those words together for any distance which you think is right for you. Enjoy!"

"I'm sorry that I called you a real piece of work, Lyon," I said, as I got up from my chair. "Allow me to clarify. I should have called you what you really are, which is a piece of flash fiction," I announced with an ear to ear, pearly white smile that only a dentist could make.

POETIC INJUSTICE

"You need to find a voice
which permeates your work,"
the literary agent proclaimed.
So I scaled from the depths of
deep to the heights of squeak,
until I ran out of genres
into laryngitis.
"I don't hear the voice," he
noted with disdain.
So I gargled my way in search
of advice anew, only to be told
that I needed to build a platform.
But when I finally stood upon
what I had built, a trap door
opened and left me hanging,
unable to even give my
verse away.

AURA LINGUA

I have spent years searching for the Muse, Aura Lingua, the golden tongued mistress of gilded words, forever glittering in the hearts and minds of readers: the woman with the Midas Touch, Elle Dorado, the Mother Lode. As any gold prospector worth his pan will tell you, finding gold is not easy, and without the golden blessing of Aura, my words would not pan out. I persevered like a Greek Argonaut traveling with Jason in search of the Golden Fleece. The more I pursued Aura, the more she seemed to be an aura: an invisible emanation, fraudulently fleecing me of all hope. I wanted the keys to punch out a golden script which was woven, not spun; with real gold, not fool's gold.

Like so many other things that I coveted, I found Aura, too, at my saloon. She looked back at me from the mirror into which I stared, as I sat on a stool drinking Prosecco at the bar. I raised my glass to her and then placed it to my lips, feeling the bubbles bursting under my nose. The golden nectar flowed through my body and soul. As I placed the glass back on the bar, I saw Aura smiling at me, as she began to fade away while blowing kisses until she was out of sight.

GOING TO THE MAT

My session with Dr. Lyon Couch built up my confidence. I began to believe in myself, even if no one else did. I knew precisely how many of my stories had been rejected: all of them. Moreover, the rising pile of rejections just kept rising higher and higher. But I had stood my ground in similar battles against interior decorators who had tried to dictate style, against sommeliers who had tried to match a specific wine with a specific food, against parents who had tried to limit my use of ketchup on anything and everything, and against restauranteurs who had tried to tie a Windsor knot in a tie that was required, but which I didn't have, and which I refused to borrow. Chacun à son goût, each to his own taste, became my literary *cri de guerre*, a battle cry that helped keep the pile of my rejected stories rising.

As I was a bit of a tree hugging, recycling oriented greener, I started to use the rejected stories and poems as place mats on the bar and tables at the saloon. One day, I overheard one of the customers characterizing my writing as "pithy." What if the man had a lisp, I wondered. Wouldn't that make the word lean toward criticism? I am like that: hearing homonyms, homophones, and homographs all around me.

"Excuse me, my good man," I called out. "I couldn't help but hear you characterize my writing as 'pithy.'"

"Yeth," the good man replied.

"Yeth, you say?," I asked, as my concern grew. "I hate to ask you this, but when you say pithy, is that the lispless form of the word, or the lispish form?"

"Well, that's a good question," he replied. "Can one actually pronounce pithy in a lithspish form?"

Assuming that he hadn't meant to say that the writing was pissy, I still felt it a pity that I wasn't sure.

My story filled place mats, which our patrons called story mats, put the saloon on the map. Prolixity Tidings, the gossip guru for the *Toonton Gazette,* noted in her column one day that "Former U.S. Vice President John Nance Garner may have thought that the Vice Presidency wasn't worth a bucket of warm spit, but the Spit at Spit Toon's Saloon is priceless; so scan his place mat stories and take them, one by one, by the tale, and see a man's life revealed with the clarity of a good claret."

So, I may not have accomplished my dream of writing the great American novel, but if there was such a thing as the great American story place mat, I believed that my mats were in contention for that title.

CHISELED WORD

A writer hangs his button-down
shirt words on an online clothesline
with keyboard clothespins,
and then he watches them
flap as if they were three
sheets to the wind.
He prays that they will
break free, hold onto
invisible handrails, and
march stutter-step toward
a blue, stone sky where
they will chisel their way
into eternal print.

ELECTRA SURGE

As the saloon's cachet rose, we started our own cabaret. And on opening night, none other than Electra Surge was the featured singer. Electra had no bigger fan than me. I had been front row center for all her Broadway musicals, as well as right in front of the piano at her cabaret gigs around town. Ever so frail, with a face as wrinkled as a theater curtain, Electra tottered slightly on her stiletto heels, but she still proved, night after night, that she was ageless, even though she talked rather than sang through a song in a hoarse and gravelly voice. She still could bring back memories from many years ago of her explosive delivery from the stage. After finishing her rendition of Kander and Ebb's "New York, New York," she started to sing their song "Cabaret." As she began the part about the death of her friend Elsie, I saw a special glow in her eyes. I only half noticed that she kept her hand on her chest, while belting out the lyrics with more gusto than I'd ever heard before. The audience gasped. She collapsed to the floor. I was the first one at her side. As I rhythmically performed CPR to the lyrics that I was hearing, but which she wasn't singing, I knew that she would not be back for an encore.

Electra's farewell wishes were very specific. She wanted to be cremated on a burning pyre on a raft floating down the river, on the banks of which the party of all parties would be held to celebrate her life. We couldn't get the approval to do it, but we did get approval for two tugboats, each connected to opposite ends of the raft by a long chain, to stabilize the raft in a fixed position, on which the pyre without a body symbolically burned. The eulogies flowed in concert with the wine. Tears and laughter blended like different flavors from noble grapes, while the music and the songs made the stars glitter like the lights of a discotheque. It was left to me to spread her ashes. I held the urn over the water, and I let the currents carry her ashes away. Stillness engulfed me. I felt tears on my cheeks. As I walked away, I wondered who would hold my urn over the water when my time came.

LAUNCH

The steeple stood tall on
a launching pad over a
simple church of stone.
A spire atop it stretched ever
higher seeking to pierce through
a membranous sky.
Time to launch ratcheted down
in cadence with the belfry's chimes,
as prayer and song, in concert with
the organ's music, lifted our
spirits.
As zero was called and ignition
achieved, I lay flowers at the foot
of your grave, under the glow
of your shuttle rising.

BROADWAY BABY

She was a Broadway baby, born
in a hospital on the Great White
Way, and nursed on the Big Apple,
whose juice still coursed through
her veins to her final day.
She learned to crawl on a stage,
where she later danced as a hoofer
in a chorus line, tapping her feet to
the beat of her heart.
At the end of her career, she left
Gotham City to retire on another
side of another city in a different
theater of the world, where she
found happiness in piano bars
and cabarets.
But on certain lonely nights,
the sound of an orchestra playing
an overture wafted toward her
from a skyscraper, mountain top.
In her mind, she saw a theater curtain
majestically rising, and a feeling of
contentment filled her soul as she heard her
heart beating to the rhythm of a chorus line's
tapping feet.

IN VINO VERITAS

It seemed like a good idea at the time, and it was the perfect place to do it. I decided that the gently sloping hill to the river bank was where I would start a vineyard. The prospect of growing my own grapes and producing my own line of Spit wines for the saloon filled me with excitement. I dreamed of calling my wines Red Spit, White Spit, Blush Spit, and Sparkling Spit, but I didn't have a clue how to begin.

I bought books, visited vineyards, and talked with owners and winemakers about what grapes to grow and which grapes to blend. The advice was inconsistent with my goal of having hardy grapes which were resistant to climate stress, animal damage, insect infestation, and any need to ever be sprayed. So, I attended viticultural and winemaking seminars, where I learned about grape pathology, trellising, pruning, weed control, fermentation, maceration, must, and ullage.

Auditioning grapes of all sizes, colors, and nationalities, I chose Seyval Blanc and DeChaunac, from central casting at a *B*-movie studio, to be my co-star grape varietals. The romantic script I penned for my two stars turned into an epic tale of jungle warfare, because birds gotta fly and deer have to eat. My vineyard was where all of Mother Nature's wine aficionados came for Sunday brunch, as well as all their other meals and snacks. Between these daily skirmishes, I tried to produce a heavenly nectar which I could enter in the first annual Spit Toon's Saloon wine tasting.

The tasting was not without controversy. Nine bottles stood proudly at attention, glistening brightly and awaiting the group's praise. My entry, a lone brown bagged bottle prominent in its contrarian bearing and labeled "Mystery Wine," stood begrudgingly to the side of the glorious contenders, each breathing deeply and rhythmically as in an oenophilic Lamaze technique.

Blupher Punditt, the president of the wine tasting club, handed out score cards instructing the members to apply ratings for each wine's color, bouquet, structure, sexual orientation, religious affiliation, and political persuasion. The members rotated fluidly around each auditioning bottle in societal synchrony, each raising crystal glassware in a Radio City, Rockettes styled leg kick for arms. The light from the windows bounced brightly about, ricocheting off each of the stemmed wine glasses in tiered levels of ascent from table to mouth. The sounds of pens scratching sonorously on the score cards filled the room with the sensation of a furious fugue.

Blupher announced the winners. The mystery wine came in fourth. Upon seeing "Spit" emblazoned on the label, along with the statement "Suspense in every bottle and a surprise in every swallow," Blupher became apoplectic.

"How dare you mock us — you pathetic, rotten, little grape pit — by bringing us your homemade swill," he screamed.

"I have your score card, Blupher," I announced, rising to my own defense. "It says, and I quote: 'The mystery wine has more sexual potency than all the other wines; however, it seems vasectomised, and thus infertile. It does not possess the lovely bouquet, sensuality, curvaceous structure, broad balance, and tinges of truffles evident in the other bottles.' It seems to me that you thought the wine respectable. Perhaps you might like to apologize to me — 'the mocking, pathetic, rotten, little grape pit who brought his homemade swill.'"

"My dear Spit, if you thought what I said about your Spit wine was complimentary, then you need to have your head examined," he counseled.

"Then why did it come in fourth, ahead of six of those other lovely and curvaceous wines?," I challenged, aggressively.

"Well, good Doctor, my colleagues obviously are fans of the mystery and horror genre. The more criminally horrific it is, the more they seem to like it."

"Touché, Monsieur," I cried, as I fell on my bottle and marked the moment when Prosecco became the house wine at Spit Toon's Saloon.

SOMMELIER

The sommelier wouldn't go away,
instead he hovered over me
trying to sell me some Viognier.
I glared at him with rosé eyes
and told him to stop telling lies
and putting on a one man show
about wines he didn't seem to know.
But being a sycophantic fool
and trying to act so very cool,
he fawned and fawned
while I yawned and yawned
in a stalemate with no end.
Finally, I switched my gears,
stood and grabbed his ears,
and whispered a single word
very precisely to be heard.
"I do not understand," he said,
a bit perplexed and turning red.
"I don't want to create an ugly scene,
but what does that word really mean?"
"But you are a sommelier," I replied.
"You should have concluded
from to what I alluded
that it is the wine I'd like to taste.
So get it for me; please make haste."
"We haven't got it oh kind sir,"
he said with an obsequious purr.
"Is there no other varietal choice?,"
he asked in a breaking voice.
"Que sera sera," I replied,
and that is when the Syrah arrived.

FRENCH FLING

High spirited bistro
bottles of bourbon,
vodka, rye, and gin
preened in the mirror
behind the bar, as they
fussed with the labels
adorning their chests.
Soon they began to strut
their stuff in a whiskey
line, brasserie parade
over outstretched arms
and empty glasses which
couldn't get their fill.
Bouillabaisse, pot-au-feu,
and cassoulet played on a
café keyboard buffet to the
melodies of Pastis, Panachet,
Sancerre, and Vouvray.
Petit fours, chocolat, tartes,
mousse, gâteaux, and crème
brûlée danced a can-can
with each swallow, and
golden drops of digestif
soothed our caffeinated,
espresso stomachs before
we bid adieu with an
un, deux, trois cheek kiss
on the City of Lights from
Le Pont Neuf over the Seine.

YOU BETCHA!

Novella Nottingham approached me in her customary inimitable manner, which never failed to make me smile.

"You know, Spit," she said in her special way with her head cocked and her left eyebrow raised, "your story mats adorn your tables like graffiti on walls. You've really cranked out a body of work with them over the years. Collectively, the story mats are a disjointed, hodgepodge picture of you: the person and your life. Your mixture of stories and poems could be a novel approach to the great American novel itch from which you suffer. Your fusion fiction, as you like to call it, would mirror the melting pot heterogeneity of our great American, polyglot nation. Have you ever considered sorting through all your nonsense and trying to transfer it from the mats on the table to place mat pages of a book?"

"Novella, whenever you do your 'You know, Spit' routine, with that long, hanging way you say 'know,' I know that I am in trouble," I confessed.

"Let's not be coy, Spit. I know that you are in the habit of betting anyone, something, on almost anything," she stated with confidence and accuracy.

"You betcha, Novella. You, of all people, know that I bet for nothing big, just for the humor and the excitement of getting the old juices flowing, as well as to bring myself to the proverbial and quintessential cutting edge of the brink. The bets are not a big deal, just a gimmick to enhance the moment. Moreover, money doesn't necessarily change hands, but post bet bragging rights and loser humiliation are, of course, de rigeur."

"Well, are you up to my challenge?," Novella pressed.

"The stakes being what?," I asked, not hiding my enthusiasm.

"Ah, that is the question, isn't it? Well, here's my proposal. You wade through the years of matted stories and conjure up a coherent, autobiographical styled tale, and then get it published somewhere. If you do, you can put my face on the dart board near the bar. If you don't, then I get all rights to all story mats: past, present, and future. I then either lose my shirt trying to succeed where you failed, or I make a bundle while all you get is glory."

"Novella, Novella, Novella," I cried with joy. How can one not love you for creating this sense of urgency to motivate me to make my dream come true. I accept your bet with pleasure, and should I lose, I will be equally happy for any success that comes your way. It's a win-win situation. You're on."

"Oh, one more thing Spit," Novella slipped by me like a slider from a Cy Young Award winning pitcher. "I don't want you to write a novel length drone in a long list of 'I did this and then did thats,' rather something a bit quirky, perhaps of novella length."

"Oh, how I love the word novella, Novella. I used to date a girl by that name," I said, with more nostalgia than I expected.

"Yes, I know her well," she said with a smile that only a dentist could have made.

TRUMP CARD

Gut instinct guffawed at
a seemingly thoughtful
decision: a choice pondered
from every circular degree,
acutely from multiple angles,
and which I believed was right.
But, alas, a cloudburst
matter-of-factly washed away
every particle of certainty,
exposing the winning trump
card that gut-instinct held in
its hand.
"Keep the faith, baby," I heard
my stomach growl, which made me
wonder if that was the highest
trump card in the deck.

BOULEVARDS

I walked along the boulevards of a warehouse lined by high rising bookcases that provided shade from the fluorescent lights above, stopping along the way to read the flash fiction words that flashed at me from the shelves. Despite my initial shyness about flashing in general, it turned out that flash fiction actually appealed to me, because I am essentially a man who needs stark simplicity in my life: no weight, no baggage, and no clutter. But ironically, I stood in a warehouse stuffed with story mats which cluttered my life and confused my psyche. The challenge to craft a coherent tale covering a long and full life in a short format, from innumerable disparate images in the album of my mind, ignited flashes of excitement and fear. And that is exactly why I had jumped at Novella's wager, because it was betting brinksmanship at its best. Even though I wasn't expected to write the next *Moby Dick,* Novella had set the bar high.

I leafed through stories that had blossomed in my mind so long ago, wondering how they really represented my life, or anyone's life. Some were first person narratives, written in a confessional style of intimacy. Others were third person narratives, written in an attributive style of distance. Either way, the voice, the face, and the name of the protagonist were controlled, embellished, veiled, or misleading. Even if the stories were reality based, they were still just stories, not textbooks. They were made up, fabricated like myths. As the former words I wrote spoke to me, I wondered whose voice I heard, whose face I saw, and whose name was mine.

It was a revelation to hear those words, from distant places and long ago times, in my voice. My eyes grew heavy, and I fell asleep in my reclining chair. I thought I heard Aura Lingua whisper "Whoa baby, what on earth have you gotten yourself into? Don't count on me for this one."

BALLAST

Saltwater tears flow
over mildewed sponge
memories and barnacle
regrets, but they fail to
carry them over the
dam in ropes of
cascading water
to a place of lost
remembrances.
They stay with me as
excess baggage, and
they serve as ballast to
keep me on the straight
and narrow course which
I try to chart as I hold
my sextant to the stars.

BOTTOM LINE

I'm always asked "What is the bottom line?,"
but usually the answer I can't refine,
because it always depends on a number of things
which move the line like it was on springs.
Up it bounces, and then it drops,
until it finally stops
in a place where you can see
just what the answer might actually be.
But it wiggles, shifts, and slides,
and on that is what the answer rides,
but usually to a setting sun
under which I'm left holding the gun.

AWAKENING

I thought I heard my name being called, but it seemed so faraway. Although it was very faint at first, the volume began to gradually rise. "Dr. Toon, Dr. Toon, are you all right?" Then I felt hands on my shoulders, shaking me as I struggled to open my eyes. The cries of my name vibrated in my ears, followed by a slap of a hand against my cheek. I saw a woman's face. Her nose was against mine, and her eyes were staring hard at me.

"Dr. Toon, it's Saliva Godiva, your dental assistant. Wake up! Novella Nottingham, your nine o'clock appointment, is here. I know that you stayed late to catch up on paperwork last night. You must have fallen asleep in the dental chair. Are you all right?"

"Saliva, is that really you? How did you get here? No one told me that you were coming. How nice to see you at the saloon, instead of at the office."

"Sal" she shouted, as I felt the sting of another slap. "Get a grip, guy!"

"Right, let me just splash some water on my face. Where's the mouthwash? Who did you say was here? Remind me to tell you about this dream I had last night," I said, as Saliva Godiva rolled her eyes at Bidday O'Shea, my dental hygienist, who was entering the room.

"I'll get Novella for you," Saliva said tersely.

I smiled at Novella, but it went unseen as I was encapsulated in my dental gown, face mask, face shield, goggles, surgical cap, and rubber gloves.

"Good morning," I said, but all she heard was a muffled, inarticulate sound from behind the barriers guarding my mouth.

"I have read your manuscript," she told me when we finally connected. "It's not what I was expecting. Just like I find it hard to understand your muffled voice coming through your face mask and shield, I find it hard to hear the real you coming through the pages. Seriously, Sal, even though I know you so well, I still don't really know the real you. You hide behind your face mask, goggles, and shield while at the same time yearning to break free. Where are you? Who are you? Where are you coming from? I think of you as a flyby tangent on a curve. Let it all hang out."

"Novella, you can call me Sal, but don't call me distant," I stated as I removed my gloves, face shield, face mask,and goggles. "I can't imagine a life without the joy of imagination. To imagine is to be free: free to go, free to see, free to hear, free to feel, free to be with, free to be apart from, free to fantasize, and free to be just downright anybody or anything — open, closed, emotional, withdrawn, serious, or silly.

"A life is lived in time and place, both real and imaginary. Myth is the metaphor of both reality and imagination. Faith bridges the gap between the two. A teller of tales, no matter how tall, has faith in listeners to make believe they believe the make-believe. I am as phony as I am real. Aren't we all? Hopefully, though, the real us is only phony in imagination. And hopefully, the imaginary makes us more real.

"Until my final at bat, the saloon remains my special place. It is with me wherever I am, wherever I go, and whomever I'm with. We all need our own personal imaginary saloon to keep us entertained while we await 'the next next,' even if it is to be the last next. So, Novella, what do you say? If you give me one more shot, I'll take another chaser. Double or nothing?"

"You're on," she said with a smile that I thought needed a touch-up, as she gave me a high five.

Her words "to let it all hang out" brought back my initial fears of flashing, but I didn't let her see me sweat. I wondered if I would ever learn to keep my mouth shut, or at least not put my foot in it.

BOOMERANGS AND HOMING PIGEONS

With Saliva Godiva and Bidday O'Shea all over me with concern that I seemed to be losing my sense of reality, I followed the medical dictum which proclaimed that a doctor who treats himself has a fool for a patient. Although I considered myself to be the father of psychedontia, a still unrecognized dental specialty which dealt with the relationship of mind and nerves to teeth and tongue, I made an appointment to see my friend and therapist, Dr. Lyon Couch, who preferred to lay on a couch while his patient sat in a chair.

"It is an honor to have 'Pater Psychedontia' as my patient," Lyon said, as he bowed with a smile only I could have made, and then he reclined on his couch.

"So, Saliva and Bidday say that you are solipsistic?"

"No, they didn't use that esoteric term, Lyon. They are concerned that the dreaming I use as an outlet to stop swimming upstream in saliva and to get out of the mouth and into the world is detaching me from reality."

"Well, is it?"

"It could, I suppose, but I think I still have all my marbles lined up in a row, but not in a way that you should diagnose as being obsessive-compulsive."

"Okay, let's just slow down, back up, and consider what we know. You escape in your dreams which, you've told me before, take you to an imaginary place called Spit Toon's Saloon: the playground of your mind and where you entertain yourself. If you are spending a disproportionate amount of time in your mental sandbox, so to speak, then you could be suffering from solipsism syndrome, which is a state of mind in which the dream world becomes real. If your mind's toggle switch gets caught in the dream position, you can get trapped in that dream world. Not only do you become detached from reality, you become a prisoner of fantasy, imagination, the unreal, or whatever you want to call it.

"The cause can be associated with environments of infinite blackness, which is how you seem to perceive the oral cavity. To stay connected to reality, you have to imagine that your imagination is a boomerang, or a homing pigeon, each with the ability to return automatically to where it started from; otherwise, you will be caught in the groove of your own bullspit forever.

"I am writing you two prescriptions, neither of which can be filled at the pharmacy. One is for the sporting goods store, for the boomerang, and the other is for the pet store, for the homing pigeon. Spit, Sal, it was good seeing you both. Spit, stay in touch with Sal. At the very least send him a postcard now and then. Oh, and maybe you should ease up on calling Samantha, Saliva; and Brooke, Bidday. And I can't remember the last time I heard you call Rinnce, Beverly. Why don't you surprise her tonight, over dinner, with her real given name. I bet your daughter Spittella would be happy to hear you call her

Carla. Sal, remember to do everything in moderation — especially your 'spittooneering.'"

I wondered if I could take credit for the term "spittooneering" and get it listed in the American Psychiatric Association's *Diagnostic and Statistical Manual of Mental Disorders.* Relieved that I was still the rational, pragmatic guy whom I'd always assumed I was, and that my bullspit toggle switch wasn't stuck in the wrong position, I felt comfortable returning to my silly, willynilly, storied style of life, where one man, in his time, plays many parts in which he becomes spitting images of himself.

OH BABY!

*Fetally curled and sucking my thumb,
making believe it was mint chewing gum,
I was content beyond all belief,
until suddenly I shrieked "Good grief!,"
as I began to move and make my way
from the darkness to the light of day.
Soon, I couldn't move anymore,
as if I'd hit a rock, solid door
which was closed and locked
so that from the goal I'd be blocked.
Finally, the door began to move,
opening up a narrow groove
through which I couldn't pass
because of my ample body mass.
Then I saw a forceps inch toward me
to grab and pull me out and free.
"No," I cried, "I'm not a tooth.
I'm a baby; it's the gospel truth."
Alas, no one listened to what I said,
and I was dragged out very hard instead
to be born an only child, sibling free,
into a world I thought was just about me.
But then some character gave me a slap,
so I let him know I didn't like that crap.
Then between my legs he grabbed a part,
and I thought he was cutting out my heart,
but it was what I think they call
the very deepest cut of all.
Oblivious to this worldly maze
in which I'm still lost in a haze,
I look back to those halcyon days
when I was fetally curled in a daze.*

ON A SAIL OF SHORT STORIES

My boat of dreams travels
over a sea with an unfurled
white sail filled with the
wind on which scenes of
my life are projected.
When they fade away, I
write untold stories on
the sail with whitewater
ink, in snaps and splashes.
And when the ink dries,
I fold the sail and carry
my short stories with me
to transcribe another day.

ON A RAFT OF POEMS

Autumnal leaves
in golden years
called me to a
river's shore, from
where I set sail to
see anew.
Through different
eyes, in different
times, a new world
appeared to me.
With brush stroked
and palette knife cut
painted words, I
drew on feelings,
imagined and real,
and on a raft of
poems I traveled
to wherever it took
me.

SCRAPED AND SHAPED

My father Luca saw his role in raising me as being a sculptor. Being an only child, raised atop an isolated hill in the country, he always looked for ways to keep me challenged and socially involved.

Although I thought Little League baseball was the obvious answer, my father, a quintessential renaissance man, thought it was "too limiting." He had succumbed to the allure of a man named Lord, for whom he had become an apostle. He dressed me in the Lord's robes: khaki knee-high socks, short pants, a neckerchief, and a wide brimmed hat. For a kid who wanted a baseball uniform, looking like the founding father of the Boy Scouts, Lord Baden-Powell, was a bit of a letdown, to say the least.

The fact that there was no Boy Scout troop in our community did not stop Luca Toon. He formed one, and as he was the founding father of the troop, as well as the Scoutmaster, my motivation to excel never waned, because his right foot was always tapping my derriere like a placekicker practicing off the tee. It was that foot that lofted me through the uprights to Eagle, and then to Lodge Chief of the Order of the Arrow, where I quickly honed my political and diplomatic skills to find ways to avoid running through the woods in a loincloth and war paint in search of the campfire around which an indian dance was being held. Everything that Scouting had to offer was served up to me, whether I wanted it or not. To this day, I still suffer anxiety when I see a picture of Lord Baden-Powell, as I remember how I traveled across our country to Philmont Scout Ranch in New Mexico dressed in those knee-high socks, short pants, a neckerchief, and that ridiculous wide brimmed hat that the Lone Ranger and no self respecting baseball player would have ever stooped to wear.

PRAY TELL

"So, Luca, have you taken Salvatore to church yet?," Reverend Godleigh Hart asked, as he had at every previous dental appointment with my father.

"No, Godleigh, not yet, just to Mother Nature's pine forest, interdenominational chapels when I take the scout troop camping. And Godleigh, please call me Luke," my father would say like every time before.

"Luke, this cannot continue. Your son has to be exposed to organized religion. He can't be kept away from the tenets of the Lord," Godleigh decreed.

"Godleigh, you know that I don't believe in organized religion. I and Lord Baden Powell impart the moral tenets upon which Salvatore can nourish his spirituality."

"Luke, as the French say, you are so *pleine de merde*. He needs God. He needs Jesus. You are failing your son, my son."

"Yeah, yeah, yeah, Godleigh, I know you're right. By the way, why do you hide behind French when you want to tell someone that he's full of shit?"

"Tell you what, Luke, I want you to start sending Salvatore to Sunday School," the good Reverend responded, ignoring my father's command of the French language. "It is absurd that your office is adjacent to my church and that you don't attend."

And so, at the age of eight, I began a journey, which I was told I needed to make, to a place about which I was unfamiliar: organized religion. My guide on the holy ship upon which I embarked was a woman named Witchia Hazelia, who would later guide me through Rome as my high school Latin teacher.

Often, after attending a church service, my parents and I would either join Reverend Hart at the Rectory, or at our house, for a long, Sunday afternoon repast. The most lasting thing I learned on those Sundays was an appreciation for the National Football League, as Reverend Hart had a television at the Rectory, which was something we didn't have at our house.

"I like to think that it was Reverend Hart's commitment to social justice that influenced me to gravitate toward anyone who was an underdog.

Although he had introduced me to the New York Giants football team, for whom everyone was a fan, I had somehow stumbled into becoming a Brooklyn Dodgers baseball fan, which classified me as a minority and a rebel. I had no choice, therefore, but to hate the all-powerful dynasty called the New York Yankees. I became a pariah among my peers. This predictably pushed me toward hooking up with the Democrats, the champions of the downtrodden, which thus made me a target for derision by my affluent, successful, establishment friends on the political right.

When the Dodgers followed the call to "Go West," leaving me holding the first base bag, I became desperate. Looking for a team to love, I latched onto the black sheep of baseball, the Mets, which further drove me away from the mainstream, as well as enlarging that bull's-eye on my forehead at which the with-it, insiders of life could take their pot shots.

Life choices like these were backing me into a corner in which I wasn't sure I wanted to be, but I couldn't help myself. Joe Namath came to town, and the Jets became my football team. I was a traitor. "How could I not do the right thing?," everyone asked. "How could I not follow the Giants?"

In a final coup of turning my back on the mainstream, I chose dentistry over medicine, driving myself deeper into the status of stepchild to the world. I have no doubt, which is really something for a guy with so much self-doubt, that these life choices planted the seeds for my vulnerability to anxiety, which then became branded deeply in my psyche, and which led me, one day, to that chair in the office of Dr. Lyon Couch.

A FOREIGN TONGUE

While my friends bantered in the living languages of the world, I was barely able to keep my head above the waters of the dead sea of Latin.

"You have been scammed, *mon ami*," the exchange student from Aix-en-Provence told me. "Latin is not the only way, or even the best way, to get a solid foundation in language. After all, as a result of the Norman Invasion, nearly 900 years ago, half of all English words are derived from French. Moreover, a large number are cognates, meaning they have the same spelling. Take the English word perspiration. The French word is identical, except that it is pronounced with a French accent to make it sound like 'purse-purr-assy-own.'"

Even lawyer and physician friends of my parents told me that whatever Latin I needed to know could be learned in thirty minutes and printed on one wallet-sized card. They told me that the myth of Latin's importance had been perpetrated as a curse by Witchia Hazelia, Caesar's nanny. It was then that I knew that the curse had been put on me, as she was stalking me in church and school.

When the dreaded witch assigned me to be the master of ceremonies at the annual Latin dinner, I did not let her see me sweat. Being an Eagle Scout, I knew what it meant to "Be Prepared," which I was when I welcomed the students. I stood tall in a toga of supreme grandeur, holding my scroll taut between two golden handles — authentic touches that my aunt, a Broadway producer, sent from Wardrobe. I read and spoke with confidence, eternally grateful that my cousin Franco, aka Brother Jesterius at the seminary, had translated my speech from English to phonetic Latin. Witchia Hazelia sat in awe, marveling at my voice ringing with a vocabulary so rich, so precise, and so idiomatic that she thought she was receiving a deliverance from a Roman deity.

She could not stop smiling at, and bragging to, the world about my triumph. She greeted me every morning with such joy and pride that my hardened image of her began to soften; however, word travels fast in a small town, as everyone knows someone. The winds of gossip opened the box in which my secret lay, carrying it in gusts, blasts, and swirls which sang the lyrics from my hidden song to the world.

Soon, Witchia Hazelia's smile was gone, her glare was cutting, and the grip of her hand clutching my throat was tight. With her *digitus medius fingerus* firmly placed between my eyes, she growled "How dare you!," to which I replied: "*Magister artis ingeniique largitor venter*."

"And what do you mean by that?," the evil witch shrieked.

"It seemed like a good idea at the time," I replied.

"Don't mess with me, kiddo," Witchia grumbled with a guttural sound that only a devil could make. "And for your information, *Spittoris Wise Assius*," she added, "the precise meaning of the phrase you so smugly spoke is 'Necessity is the mother of all invention.'"

I wished I could fall on my sword, but I had already returned it to my aunt.

THE KING'S ENGLISH

We used to travel wide and far
on our own in a rented car,
but as we got older, it became exhausting,
in addition to how much it was costing.
We drove on the wrong side of the road, and
our suitcases became too much of a load.
We were always lost and always late,
missing a date and relying on fate.
We struggled with the native tongue of
the people with whom we were among.
Finally we switched to an escorted tour,
as it seemed the best way to be safe and sure.
Our flight was met by a knowledgeable guide,
who led us for a choreographed ride
with fellow travelers of the English tongue
from the Commonwealth widespread and far-flung.
Although English is English, it was unfamiliar,
as many of the words and sounds were not similar
to the way in which we had been taught.
So in the confusion in which we were caught,
we resorted to ad-libbed gestures of the hand,
but into trouble it was very easy to land.
Although idioms, slang, and vernacular
make conversations truly spectacular,
a different finger for a different zinger
leads to a misunderstanding which tends to linger.
Words like bingle, bonzer, chook, and baccy
seemed to us Yanks a wee bit tacky,
but by any other name a rose
smells the same to the nose,
I suppose.

MAESTRO

A beleaguered, unhappy member of the high school band was I. In fact, I just downright hated being a part of it. I was there only because I wasn't a jock, but then again, I wasn't a musician either. In fact, I had no musical talent, whatsoever. Rhythm and beat were two concepts I could not grasp. Even the curvaceous, blonde clarinet player could tell you what deadweight I was on the dance floor. But I needed to be able to list some extracurricular activities on my college applications and, as my parents played bridge regularly with the head of the music department, band was one of them.

I went through the motions of playing the trumpet, but you'd be hard pressed to recognize the sound that came out of it. Yes, I did know how bad I was. In fact, I considered myself to be the spit valve of the organization.

I was, and I still am, one of those guys who can't chew gum and walk at the same time. So, you can imagine the challenge I faced trying to play the trumpet and march on the playing field at half-time. I had to concentrate intently on not turning the wrong way at the wrong time, or I would crash into the sousaphone player. So, I faked playing my horn. For lack of a better term, I guess you could say that I horn-synched and fudged.

So, it was quite a surprise when I, the consensus worst player in the band, was unanimously nominated for, and elected as, president of it. My theory was that no one else wanted the job, so everyone mobilized to stick the title on me in a tsunami wave of support, and as a bad joke. One of the many troublesome realities of being the band president was that when we gave concerts, I had to be the student conductor of it. Remember now, I was the guy who had no sense of rhythm or beat. So, in politically charged, smoke-filled backrooms with the band members, I used my newly gained political clout to make sure that they ignored my waving baton and just followed each other. The emotional scars of standing before my colleagues, with an audience behind me as I waved my baton meaninglessly, still remains to this very day.

But here's the thing. By being elected president of the band, I was perceived to have a political persona, and I was nominated to run for Student Council Treasurer, and then Student Council President. All of a sudden, I was immersed in politics. As Student Council President, I was meeting regularly with the principal, a very intimidating guy who dismissed my input with such cavalier disdain that I got my music stand up. Bingo, my political petals blossomed on a thorny stem. It didn't take long to figure out how, when, where, and on whom to use the petals or the thorns so as to never be off-key on any issue.

FUDGE

Salvatore, then Spit, has been my name,
but since I'm wobbly in the numbers' game,
I've also been called Fudge,
a moniker for which I hold no grudge.
I like to think I'm smart enough,
but numbers bore me, and I find them tough.
"Close enough" is my well-known cry,
as I fudge my calculations to just get by.
One day I found myself romantically hooked,
and before I knew it the wedding was booked.
My bride thought she had my number,
but it didn't take her long from
that belief to disencumber,
because I rarely get a number right,
even if it's close in sight,
unless it refers to one special thing,
which to the punch line now does us bring.
It's actually pretty ironic, as well as quite funny,
but if I'm owed, I'm right on the money
to every single decimal point exact,
although at times with a lack of tact.
It's gotten me into a few sticky wickets
and trapped me in a number of thickets,
but most of all, it has kept me in a chocolate sludge,
guaranteeing that I'll always be called Fudge.

THE FACT OF THE MATTER

If it looks, sounds, and tastes like fizz,
it really shouldn't take a whiz
to realize that the fact of the matter is
that it is what it is, namely fizz.
This brings me to the matter at hand,
about this phrase heard throughout the land,
that people are wont to bandy about
to create the feeling that they have clout.
And the phrase to which I refer, and
about which I feel too many err,
especially when it's on a quiz,
is "the fact of the matter is."
Even if you say it, you might still
be in arrears, because what you think
is fact may not be what it appears.
In fact, actual fact may be packed in a
box labeled "Knowledge You've Lacked."
What you perceive is all well and good,
but that doesn't mean that you should
assume that it is the be-all and end-all,
or in others' opinion you may fall.
In fact, you might be as mad as a hatter
to believe what you hear is
"the fact of the matter."

WORDPLAY

It didn't take me long to realize that Luca NMI Toon and his lovely wife, Sally Spittell Toon, were double covering me to ensure that they could deflect or intercept any threatening situations. My father was resolute in making sure I developed confidence, a strong character, a good work ethic, social graces, and leadership skills. My mother was in charge of developing my facility with words. So while my father was kicking me in the derriere to move up the Boy Scout hierarchy, my mother was telling me tales about my uncle who "memorized" the dictionary and who read every page of the *Encyclopedia Britannica* by his tenth birthday. And like a football practice, she would run me through my paces on a Scrabble board and a Jotto pad.

I liked Scrabble, but I loved Jotto. Each player tried to be the first to guess the other player's secret five letter word. Five letter test words were exchanged. The player asking the test word was told how many letter matches it had to the secret word. Even if you were the first to solve the five letter match, you still needed the correct sequence of letters to win. The art of the game was to eliminate unused letters, to confirm used letters, to determine whether a letter appeared more than once, and to pick the right sequence of the five letters before the opponent guessed yours. I was ecstatic the first time I heard my mother declare me the winner with the exclamation "Jotto!"

To this day, I still play Jotto in down moments with anyone I can find. If they don't know the game, I teach it to them on any make-do scrap piece of paper. In college, there were a few students who could play Jotto without paper and pencil. They would exchange rapid sequences of verbal exchanges without any visual crutches. I never rose to that level of competence and showmanship.

But one reaps what one sows, and my parents reaped a child whom I would call prolix, but whom they believed was afflicted with oral diarrhea.

WALTER DITTY

I was called Walter Ditty
as I was thought to be a Walter Mitty,
that fictional character who dreamed wild things
with an imagination that was launched on springs.
I'd always had a penchant for pun and rhyme
as far back as I could remember to another time.
I'd penned my share of ditties, doggerel, and verse
which some believe I still will be doing in my hearse.
It started in high school passing notes
to lovely young damsels seeking their votes,
and when they giggled right out loud,
I knew I had them, and I was on a cloud.
I was known for content which some said was great,
and for meter that most said was below cut rate.
It appeared not to matter the least bit at all,
as for it the damsels seemed to fall.
And after college while on the job,
I met the girl with whom I wanted to hobnob,
so I penned my stuff and passed it along,
expecting to hear her laughter and song,
but she looked at me with deep disdain
and told me to not a poet feign.
Jolted by this dismissal rare,
I began to write again with much more care,
dropping my meter, rhyme, and wordplay,
and hoping that she would not say nay.
And indeed an affirmative response I got,
and I became a romantic, literary, poetic hotshot.
But alas my poetic heat turned cold real quick,
so with the ditties I did stick.

BODY OF WORK

A child stood before her class
and read a poem which she had written,
by herself, without help, and from her
heart. Every eye and ear honed in on
what she said. Tears of joy and sadness
clapped against each other to celebrate
her words.
She took to heart the rules of language
that were metered out along the way,
leading to the mastery of her mother
tongue. Carried forward in her studies
on blanket clouds of metaphor and
prosody, she pushed against the
envelope of joy in which she breathed
poetic air, until the worded walls
crumbled under her pen.
A poet laureate stood in a regal pulpit
before a clamoring throng. The aura
of her acclaim and heralded body of
work glistened like military ribbons,
or merit badges on a sash. Every eye
and ear honed in on the experimental,
alternative styles for which she was
known. There were no tears of joy or
sadness, only closed eyes and nodding
heads.

"MUMBLES"

We called him "Mumbles," because that's all we heard when he spoke, which was rarely. In fact, mum was the word in my third year high school social studies class. Mumbles would just sit on the front of his desk, rubbing his hands, and swinging his feet which didn't reach the floor. No one looked more overwhelmed with life than he. It took us a few days to get the hang of his style, which was the absence of any style, whatsoever.

We would take our seats at which there was a copy of either the *New York Herald Tribune* or the *New York Times*. He would be sitting on his desk, occasionally mumbling something inaudible or incoherent. Then he would gaze at us with watery eyes before finally just staring down at the floor. We would sit there quietly, not sure what to make of it or what to do. In that perpetual vacuum, it was inevitable that we would start to look through the newspapers on our desk. At first we would just turn the pages, one by one, looking at the advertisements. The girls finally stumbled upon the fashion, style, food, and entertainment sections to which they began to look forward to each day. The guys found their way to the sports section at which most of them stayed. I kept moving around everything until I stumbled upon a page called "Op-Ed."

In the beginning, I thought it was some journalist's by-line. I started reading a column that had a photo of the columnist at the top. He was a funny looking guy, and he wrote very funny stuff. His name was Art Buchwald, and I became a fan. I couldn't wait to get to class to see how the world looked through his eyes. But one Art Buchwald column did not a full hour take, so I started to read the column next to his by a guy named Joseph Alsop. To my surprise, I liked him too, even though he wasn't funny. Soon I was reading Russell Baker, who was funny, and Scotty Reston, who wasn't. One day, I slipped on the crease between the op-ed page and the editorial page and discovered new horizons. It was no surprise that my renaissance father, who at first was horrified by my initial reports about the class, was delighted to witness my love for those two world class newspapers.

Looking back, I now believe that those 750 word columns I read daily were what predisposed me to flash fiction and storied place mats. I've always felt guilty about how I held poor Mumbles in such low regard, but in fact, he made a big difference in my life. There are two things I need to start my day now: a glass of orange juice and the *New York Times,* both of which I get most mornings by walking to the the coffee shop on the corner. I tell my friends that I walk for the morning newspaper — not for the news — but to renew myself.

F. SCOTT

My mother called to me through the kitchen window that dinner was ready. I was throwing a tennis ball against the concrete wall of our detached garage, and then fielding the rebounds, throwing out imagined runners, and calling a nine inning game in my mind.

"Why on earth do you spend so much time throwing a ball at a wall, Salvatore?," my father asked as I entered the dining room.

"It's over compensation for having been denied the opportunity to play Little League, Dad," I answered with a smile that he knew only a dentist's son could make. "And, Mom, Dad, call me Spit. That's what I go by now."

"Spit? Are you out of your mind? Who ever heard of such a name? How on earth did you come up with that?," they both said in unison and despair.

"Mom, Dad, slow down. Deep breath. Count to ten. Relax. I can explain."

"No one could explain such a thing," my mother said.

"Of all the names out there, you pick Spit," my father groaned.

"One sec; I'll be right back," I announced.

I scampered up to my bedroom, grabbed the book, and scooted back into the dining room.

"I'll explain, as we enjoy Mom's wonderful cooking," I announced confidently, but they both just sat there staring at me with sad eyes and no appetite. "Okay, okay," I cried, as I put my fork down and picked up the book.

"Today, in English, my teacher announced that each of us was to choose an American author whose major works we would read, and whom we would periodically impersonate through the course of the school year. We all went to the school library to research the choices. Everyone was looking for an author who wrote the fewest, shortest, and easiest works. My classmates who ran track found them first. Well, I decided on F. Scott Fitzgerald, and I've already learned that he used his middle name as his first name. So,as I'm now immersing myself into his psyche and persona, I've decided to use my middle name as my first name; however, I've shortened your maiden name, Mom, to create a more masculine image, because I didn't think Spittell worked as a first name."

"You will always be Salvatore to me," my mother said.

"Dad?," I asked.

"Spit, I'm glad to meet you," he announced after a long pause, as he rose from his chair, walked over to me, and stuck out his hand.

My mother broke down and cried.

On the last day of the school year, my classroom was filled with students impersonating famous American novelists. For me, this was the easiest and most enjoyable day of the year, because I had morphed into F. Scott Fitzgerald on the very first day of class by beginning to read everything that Fitzgerald had written, as well as beginning auditions to find my Zelda. On that memorable last day, I strutted into the classroom dressed to the nines, with a martini glass in my hand and Zelda on my arm.

Years later, I found one of my Fitzgerald periodic reports in a drawer of my father's desk. My teacher had sent it with the following comment scrawled across the top: "Pretentious little bastard, isn't he?"

"KAYMUSS"

It turns out that F. Scott had something contagious, and I caught it. According to my father, it wasn't an infection, but rather a psychosomatic vulnerability to a condition known as "Great American Novelitis."

"Is it serious?," I asked, cluelessly.

"Oh, yes, my son, very serious. It will haunt you until your final day. You will have an addict's never satisfied yearning for something you will never achieve."

And it was with that sense of hopelessness that I entered my first day of English class in my senior year of high school, where I was introduced to a French author whose name my teacher pronounced as "Al Burt Kaymuss." As I was mired in my fourth year of Latin, aka "Deadspeak," I didn't realize that the proper pronunciation was "Al Bare Kammoo." Fortunately, the student sitting beside me in class was the curvaceous, blonde clarinet player from band. She was in her fourth year of French, and when she stopped laughing at the teacher's lingual faux pas, she berated him unmercifully. I felt sorry for the guy, because I knew what it felt like to be the object of her disdain, having stepped on her toes so many times on the dance floor.

It didn't take long for me to realize that I was now between a rock and hard place, wedged between a martini glass and a croissant, and caught between competing hero worship. Not only had I contracted "Great American Novelitis" from F. Scott, but I had contracted the "Sisyphus Syndrome" from "Al Bare."

"You're making it twice as bad as it really is," my therapist explained, years later. "Your burden of 'Great American Novelitis' is just the spitting image of Sisyphus's boulder. So, you've only got one degree of hopelessness, not two. Double infinity is still infinity."

"So, when the great Gatsby looks into the mirror, whom does he see: himself or Sisyphus?," I asked my mentor of the mind.

"The same person we all see when we look into a mirror," he replied.

ASTERISK

It was in my dreams that I caught the bug, which I couldn't dismiss with just a shrug, because it took hold of me hard and deep each night when I went to sleep. It called on me to write the book which had the very magic hook for which authors drool and grovel, known as "the great American novel."

First I looked for the perfect niche, but each one seemed to have a hitch, as they were all so small and filled, and not at all what they'd been billed. A genre then was what I sought, and which I gave much serious thought, but not a single one did ring my bell, as I didn't believe I had much to tell.

I prayed for help to let my words go free, and then miraculously the answer came to me. It was so obvious and easy to see. The challenge I had shattered. It was the title that mattered.

I had never felt so slick or sage as when I wrote atop the page my asterisked title: The Great American Novel. I put the asterisk there just to keep it fair and square by acknowledging that it was not the real thing, but only doggerel by a dreamer on a fling.*

SAD SONGS AND FUNNY TALES

Drinking some imported ales
in my boat of masts and sails,
under seagulls' cries and wails,
is a respite which never fails
to rid me of my inner gales.
And under still and starry skies,
I dream in peace until I rise
and place my sails to the wind
to ensure that my cares I do rescind.
But on one very stormy night,
in a dream I had a horrid fright
that my boat was about to capsize
from white capped waves on the rise.
A great white whale was approaching fast,
remembering my flavor from a meeting past.
I grabbed my leg and it wasn't there.
I only had one, not a pair.
Then I felt the whale on me,
which made me afraid to open my eyes to see,
but fingers pried open each, one by one.
They were the fingers of my young grandson.
Up and about Ahab, my wife ordered loudly,
and to her command I responded proudly
to begin a new day with unfurled sails
while listening to sad songs and funny tales.

THE HINTERLAND

I was itching to scale the ivy covered walls of higher education, and my high school English teachers guided me through the hinterland to Hinterland College, a tradition reeking, small, elite, liberal arts, all-male bastion plopped high on a hill in the middle of nowhere, where 800 horny men were constantly on the prowl for coeds at other schools. What was I thinking? All I can say is "Magister artis ingeniique largitor venter?" which I still believe means "It seemed like a good idea at the time," despite Witchia Hazelia's contention to the contrary.

I had never actually decided that I wanted to be a dentist, but I had always assumed that I would be. So, I majored in all the pre-med sciences. Hinterland had a rigorous curriculum distribution requirement which required me to take a foreign language, philosophy, English, economics, history, and four years of public speaking. The laboratory time involved with the sciences made it difficult to really dig into the other courses, which I really enjoyed.

In my third year of French, the chairman of the French Department offered me a ride as I walked down the hill to the village. He asked if I was taking a foreign language, to which I diplomatically indicated that not only was I taking French, but that I was in his class. The professor looked at me in disbelief, asking my name, once again.

"*C'est extraordinaire*," he said. "You scored the highest grade on the final exam. Who are you? Where have you been? Why don't I know you?"

I explained that I was a science major and that the long hours I had to spend in the science laboratories impacted on my ability to maintain a higher profile in my elective courses.

"*C'est dommage*, Speet," the professor said, which I took to mean, "You poor bastard!"

I loved French, especially because my tongue was no longer being stomped upon by a Latin witch. I had hoped to spend my junior year abroad in France, but I had been offered an early admission to dental school.

Late for my genetics class one morning, I rushed across campus only to be snagged by a lone upperclassman on a soap box who berated me for being ignorant and uncaring about America's involvement in Vietnam. He was a guy whom I knew only casually, and I didn't have time to debate foreign policy with him. Not only was I late for class, but I was going to have to explain how I had let all the fruit flies in the genetics lab escape the night before, which forced me to try fudging the data on my experiment. I feared that my professor, as well as failing me, would be looking to remove some of my genes, which I held near and dear, from my body in some horrific manner. So, considering the circumstances, why should or would I question what the "Land of the Free and the Home of the Brave" was doing in Vietnam, wherever the hell that was. Certainly, the American government knew more than I did about some faraway place that wasn't my biggest problem that day. I assumed that my Uncle Sam was doing the right thing. Little did I know how wrong I was, as well as how much that moment would take hold of me one day.

GENREally SPEAKING

Looking for a course that was an easy ride, I learned that the History of Art had the strongest shock absorbers in the curriculum, as well as being a lock for a radiant *A* on my transcript. So, tilting my beret a paintbrush hair to the left, I joined the parade to Professor Hugh Bright's classroom. The litany of descriptive words that would be needed to paint a portrait of this colorful man could not be contained on an average size artist's palette.

"Half of the final grade will be based on writing a paper on an example of 'genre art,' and the other half will be based on the final exam," Professor Bright announced, then adding that the definition of genre art was for each student to learn on his own.

I asked my English professor for his take on "genre art," but all the professor said was "Oh, how I love the word genre; I used to date a girl by that name." He didn't give me the answer I was looking for, but I never forgot that line. The input from others came framed in the patois of "art-speak," hanging in oxymoronic abstract clarification, thus leading me to conclude that anything, whether it was a framed, blank canvas or a lonely, colored dot on any kind of surface, was representative of some artistic genre.

That evening, while writing a note on a humorous contemporary greeting card to the curvaceous, blonde clarinet player from high school, a girl named Novella, I had my "Eureka" moment: the card was an example of "genre art." Figuring that Professor Bright would be very impressed by such a bold, unique, and creative take on the assigned topic, I dove deep into the waters of research in search of the origin, artistic aspects, and cultural impact of the humorous contemporary greeting card. Trucks clogged the byways of the quadrangle as they delivered crates of sample cards, reams of information about the card industry, corporate reports, and buckets of Madison Avenue social science gobbledygook. When I finished writing my report, I humbly believed that it was a tour de force, shaded with just the right nuanced brush strokes. I was certain that the good professor would be pleased; however, he proved me wrong, very wrong.

"Toon, I can't think of anything I hate more than these asinine cards," Professor Bright told me. "I will admit that you wrote a terrific paper, arguably the best ever submitted to me; however, because I detest, so intensely, these culturally reprehensible pieces of folded cardboard, with their moronic prose and cartoon smears, I am only giving you a grade of *B*.

The shocks on this easy riding artistic vehicle were not living up to the hype I had been given. I was finding that the pot holes of "Palette Parkway" were bouncing me around as if I were a basketball being dribbled by Degas.

Deciding that I could utilize my time more effectively if I just skipped Professor Bright's lectures and memorized history's masterpieces on my own, I showed up for the final exam cocksure and loaded with visions of the Masters. As Professor Bright flashed a series of slides on the screen, my confidence rose with each succeeding slide.

"Bacchus and Ariadne," by Titian, housed in the National Gallery in London, I wrote for the first slide.

"The Night Watch," by Rembrandt, housed at the Rijksmuseum in Amsterdam, I wrote for the second.

The succeeding slides were a Monet from Musée de l'Orangerie, an El Greco from Museo del Prado, a Turner from the National Gallery in London, and a de Kooning from the MoMA in New York.

I took a deep breath of satisfaction. Lost in the glory of my masterful recognition of the Masters, I didn't process completely the droning from Professor Bright. Panicking, I raised my hand.

"Pardon me, Professor, but I was just muffling a sneeze, so I didn't quite catch everything you just said. Could you please repeat that, sir?," I asked, mournfully, as my confidence level headed south like thin paint running down a canvas.

"Of course, my good man," Professor Bright said, with a smile that I took not as mischievous, but malicious. "I said that if you identified all of the slides correctly, you only need to answer one of four more questions to get an *A*, which should be quite simple if you attended the lectures.

"Name my favorite bistro around the corner from Musée du Louvre. Name my favorite pub across the street from the National Gallery. Name the color of the wall tiles at my favorite tapas bar next door to Museo del Prado. Name the London musical that I saw after viewing what painting, about which I made a very important point in one of my lectures?"

The proverbial rock and a hard place started to press against me, pushing closer and closer to each other while oblivious to my presence between them. I picked up my pen. My hand shook as I wrote the following Hail Mary pass styled answer: "Knew the paintings, artists, and venues; the course was not about bistro and pub menus. The color of the tapas tile could not have been true, as the lighting changed its natural hue. *Sunday in the Park with George* was the show to see; George Seurat's pointillism it had to be."

Smugly scanning my answer sheet which I had handed to him, Professor Bright's sense of self-satisfaction suffocated me like a wet, heavy blanket, as he glared at me with eyes shooting, not daggers, but palette knives.

"Toon, you're an irritating little bugger, and you're way too clever for your own good, as well as for my tolerance. I take great satisfaction in not giving you an *A*, but even more satisfaction in giving you a *C*. It will not only be a dark image on the canvas of your transcript, but a representation of my grading system, which, like contemporary cards, can be viewed as a type of genre art."

PASSE PARTOUT

Bright, dry, strokes of
multicolored water lay
on an artist's mat.
They strained to shine
through a window of
glass to flaunt their
plumage proudly.
But trapped in a pouting
passe-partout, and
sternly rebuked by their
frame, they lowered their
faces and hid from my
view, ashamed .
I rushed to their aid and took
them away to a wall without
color in my home. I passed on
using a passe-partout, and I
flung the frame far away.
Now, the bright, dry strokes of
multicolored water lay on an
artist's mat, free to flaunt their
plumage without fear, rebuke,
or shame.

SHIVER OF EXCITEMENT

A strained, single wire struggled
to hold a picture frame which was
putting a choke hold on a painting which
was in a swoon and headed for the canvas.
Disparate artistic styles faced off against
one another in the framed arena rebuking
eclecticism and the centripetal call for synergy.
A palette knife gob of retreating yellow sun
cowered in a canvas corner as swarming
dots of pointillism stampeded toward it over
the canvas plain.
Heat from the sun melted the antagonists
into brush stroke streams that
flowed to the mouth of an eddy created
by drippings and splash from a can.
A dismayed canvas gave the impression
of dark thoughts, but it was only the shadow
of the newly blended colors casting their
shade and spreading a shiver of excitement.

CADUCEUS

The School of Dental Medicine opened its "open wide, please" arms in welcome, and I shivered with excitement at having traded the male only hinterland for urban coeducation and culture. My father took great pride in "the totally independent decision" of his only child to follow in his father's footsteps by attending his dental alma mater.

Having survived the rigors of being a science major at Hinterland, I smoothly made my way over the hurdles of the basic sciences. My biggest hurdle, it turned out, was that issue of Vietnam that George Grumman had been harping about on his soapbox at Hinterland. The Army, the Navy, and the Air Force all wanted a piece of me; however, I was reluctant to let them have one. They settled for a signed piece of paper which confirmed that I would fulfill my military active duty obligation starting the day after I graduated from my four years of dental training. And so, sign I did, so that I wouldn't run the risk of being drafted from private practice at a later date.

One of my classmates moonlighted at a men's clothing store downtown, along with a number of moonlighting school teachers whom he rated an eleven on a zero to ten scale of drop-dead gorgeous. He encouraged me to stop by the store for an introduction, which I did one day. And that is where I met Rinnce, whose name now flashes in neon lights with mine at "Spit Toon's Saloon: Rinnce and Spit Toon, Proprietors."

I couldn't help but notice the two lovely young ladies tending the tie counter, as I entered Manly Threads, the fanciest men's clothing store in town. Deciding that lunch with one of them would be a far, far better thing than a beer with my classmate, which was my original intention, I approached the counter. They each wore a name tag. One said Rinnce, the other Mary.

"I'm looking for underwear," I said with a smile that a dental student was learning to make.

"Boxers or briefs?," Rinnce inquired politely.

"Briefs," I replied, "but please, let's not try to profile me based on that information alone."

"Fair enough," she said reassuringly, while Mary giggled. "What size do you need?"

"Do I have to answer that?," I asked, as they both turned red.

"Medium is always a safe answer," Mary suggested.

"I do want to be comfortable, though," I said with a smile, as their redness deepened. "Okay, I'll take a dozen. Can you monogram them?," I asked.

"I don't know?," Rinnce answered. "No one has ever asked me that question before. Mary, what do you think?"

"What kind of monogram?" Mary asked.

"Here, let me show you," I said, as Mary put her hands over her eyes. This is the monogram," I said proudly, as I pointed to the dental caduceus on the pocket of my dental tunic.

"And where on your briefs would you like that monogram?," Rinnce inquired calmly, without missing a beat.

"Please, just tell us; don't show us," Mary pleaded, just before I made it clear where I wanted the age old sign of medicine placed, by pointing to the waistband on the underwear in the cellopane package on the counter.

"So, Rinnce, may I buy you lunch?," I asked, nervously.

"Now? Where? Oh, I don't know. Mary, what do you think?"

"If you don't go, I will," Mary said, eyeing me in a way that made me even more nervous.

"I'd be delighted," Rinnce decided.

"Do you know a good place close by, Rinnce?," I asked, as I raised my umbrella as we walked out the door of Manly Threads into the rain.

THE MOIRAE

The name on the door of the restaurant was Destiny. I felt a queasiness in my stomach that only the Moirae, those mythological Greek, white-robed goddesses, also known as the Fates, could stir. My anxiety rose as I realized that Destiny's hostess, who was leading us to a table in a quiet corner, was draped in a white robe.

"Having already sized you up, Spit, I think I'll have the short ribs," Rinnce announced with a grin.

"That was quick," I said, barely having opened my menu.

"Well, you did choose briefs over boxers, didn't you?," she said, giggling.

It was then and there, at that moment in a restaurant named Destiny, that the queasy sense of fate, which I was feeling in my gut, put its nose to mine and left me in no doubt as to where we were headed.

"I'll tell you about my name, if you'll tell me about yours?," I said, sheepishly.

"You'll show me what, if I show you what?," she exclaimed, feigning shock.

"Well, I do think that we might enjoy ourselves more if we got our names straight, don't you?," I replied, as I heard the Moirae turning the key in the lock of destiny's door.

"You really know how to spit on the flickering flames of passion, good doctor," she snapped back, like a winning volley over the net and down the line.

"Shall I unveil my name first, or would you like to unveil yours first?" I challenged.

"I haven't really kept abreast of these aspects of etiquette," she countered, "so, I shall defer to your preference."

"Thank you, Mademoiselle," I said with the flourish of a bow, even though I was sitting, "but *s'il vous plaît*, a gentleman always defers to the lady."

"Spit, I know you're going to find this weird, but it seems that 'the Big Molar in the Sky' may be trying to tell us something. You see, my full name is Rinnce Brush Wehl. Although it may sound like the mantra for dental health, it's really my true name. My father, Bourne Wehl, is of Irish descent. He wanted me to have an authentic Irish first name. Knowing that the American dance, the Virginia Reel, had its origins from an old Irish peasant dance called Rinnce Fadha, he and my mother chose Rinnce for my first name. Brush was my Mother's maiden name and Wehl, of course, is my father's last name."

The sound of many keys jangling and many locks turning rang in my ears.

"Rinnce, I am not a religious man, but when the power of 'the Big Molar in the Sky' makes itself known to an aspiring dentist like me, who am I to take issue?

"My full name is Salvatore Spittell Toon," I said, reaching across the table and putting my hand over hers. "My mother's maiden name was Spittell, but please call me Spit; everyone does, except my mother who still calls me Salvatore."

And with that, as we looked into each other's eyes, I saw our mutual destiny as clearly as I heard the song "On a Clear Day You Can See Forever," from the Broadway show of the same name, which had held me captive two years before in a flight of dreams that, on this day, came true.

On Valentine's Day, only five months after the Moirae had conspired with Cupid, I slipped a diamond ring on Rinnce's outstretched finger.

"Spit, we have to call my parents," she said.

"Why?"

"To tell them."

"You can show them the ring when you get home," I said, cluelessly, not callously.

"No Spit, you have to tell my father now."

"Why?"

"Spit, you didn't even ask him for my hand in marriage."

"Why would I do that?"

"It's what you're supposed to do."

"Maybe a few hundred years ago," I observed, "but hey, this is now. I'm not marrying him; I'm marrying you. Even if he didn't approve, I'd still go forward with the marriage. Wouldn't you?"

"Yes, but let's call him now, anyway," she said, as she flashed a smile that did not need a dentist's improvement.

THE EYES HAVE IT

I met her voice before I
met her eyes, because I
was on my knees dealing
with shoestring ties.
But when I rose to my full
height, I lost her voice, but
I found her sight.
I only heard what I did see
in those sky blue eyes with
which she looked at me.
The only sound that filled
the air came from the ocular
words of a smitten pair.
And when it is time to say farewell,
after a long and happy life,
we both will say our good-byes
through our verbal, loving eyes.

WHEELBARROW ANGST

While curled in the fetal position in a one wheeled,
two handled, wheelbarrow womb, sucking my
thumb and feeling pretty sorry about myself and
my failure to find love, someone slipped up behind
me, lifted the handles, and took me for a ride.
The wheelbarrow came to a screeching halt and the
supports under the handles failed to lay claim to
stability. They wavered in concert with
the palpitations of my heart until my conveyance
collapsed with a crash and rolled me face down
into the ground.
"You didn't move," the goddess cried. "I had
to push you aside."
"I'm so terribly sorry," I said forlorn,
to which she replied "You certainly are."
Frozen she stood, frozen I lay, caught in a lingering
stare, until the heat of the moment began to melt the
ice in-between.
Ever so slightly, she began to smile, as did I. She
offered a hand which I gladly grasped to be pulled out
of my wheelbarrow angst.
As the wheelbarrow shroud that had encased me for too
long peeled from my body and set me free, I bounced
with the delight of a prince at a ball.
"Slow down, slow down," she said. "You're going to sink
the boat."
But the boat didn't sink, and we set sail together on a
wonderfully wheelbarrowish whirl.

LE NOZZE DI RINNCE AND SPIT

I preferred that we elope and have a civil ceremony, but my position never made it out of committee for a vote on the floor. And it didn't take long for everyone to tire of me humming Mozart's *The Marriage of Figaro* every time wedding plans were discussed.

Rinnce's father insisted that the ceremony take place at the family church and be officiated by Father Heddin Cloud, who was very old, very tired, and very traditional. Not only could I not relate to him, but Father Cloud could not relate to me, so resorting to a Hail Mary pass style of decision-making, I called my cousin, now Father Jesterius, to officiate the ceremony at the University Chapel.

Predictably, my cousin's ceremony was slightly askew from tradition. The guests laughed quite heartily at his stories about me and the extended family Toon. I knew that my father-in-law was struggling mightily to avoid a public meltdown as "Holy Cuz," as I called my cousin, relished the opportunity to enhance his persona as a comic cleric. When he revealed that I was wont to refer to myself as "Sir Spit, paragon of goodness and virtue, and Christlike in nature," there was a schizophrenic tension in the pews toggling between gasp and guffaw. The revelation that my mother had, on occasion, played dirty word Scrabble with the principal of my high school had eyes rolling like spilled marbles.

But Bourne Wehl held up well and stood proudly outside the five star restaurant in center city, at which he had dropped a bundle, to receive the praise and appreciation of the guests as they began to wend their way home.

THE WILD BLUE YONDER

Waiting to board my flight to DaNang, Republic of Vietnam, I stood motionless in front of the television screen, stunned at what and whom I was seeing. Pearce Paxton, a classmate from Hinterland College, was on his back, wrapped in white, arms and legs connected to pulleys at different heights, and his left eye covered. He was part of an interview about injured soldiers.

"The poor guy was right about everything. No one believed him, not even me," Pearce said to the reporter, referring to George Grumman's lonely vigil atop his soapbox on the Hinterland campus.

My eyes watered as I remembered how I too had batted away George's pleas, as if they were fruit flies from the genetics lab. I tried to remember my favorite Latin phrase about something seeming like a good idea at the time, but the Latin words did not come back to me, just as the missing fruit flies never returned either. What I did remember, though, were my three weeks of basic training from which I still had nightmares of my Uncle Sam's Dracula-like teeth sinking deeply into my shoulders, while pawed looking hands pressed silver Captain's bars into the bloody holes.

My head snapped back against the airplane seat into which I was being strapped. When I arrived in Vietnam, a dental drill was slapped into one hand, and extraction forceps into the other. There I stood, for 369 days, chained to a dental chair in which another airman always was waiting to sit. While others waded through rice paddies and dense, dangerous jungles, I swam upstream in saliva in my theater of battle: the small, dark, wet, malodorous, confined space of the oral cavity.

DOOM

Being tethered to constant danger on a world stage in a theater of battle wasn't doing my psyche any good. I needed to be entertained. I needed to laugh. Being chained to my dental chair for long periods of time to shuck and fill teeth may have been improving the smiles of others, but not mine. My sense of doom was becoming overwhelming. I felt like I was falling deeper and deeper into a black hole.

It didn't help when Cutter Hack, a wonderful surgeon with an unfortunate name, invited me to join him for dinner at the Officer's Club to which I had not yet been. As we approached the white door, I saw four large black letters spelling DOOM. My anxiety level rose, but I tried to not let Cutter see me sweat.

"Hell of name for an Officer's Club," I observed, as casually as I could.

"No, it's just an acronym for DaNang Officer's Open Mess," Cutter explained.

And it was there, at that moment, on the other side of the world, treading water in saliva swamps, that I rewired my brain to perceive DOOM as the revered Algonquin Hotel in Manhattan to which my parents would drag me, hanging onto the tails of their overcoats as they jumped onto the wheels of a getaway weekend to the "Big Apple," to escape the ennui of rural living, with a bouillabaisse blend of Broadway, bistros, baseball, ballet, museums, opera, cinema,concerts, circuses, and cabaret.

The Algonquin was famous for its Round Table luncheon meetings, many years ago, of columnists, humorists, authors, actors, and playwrights. For many years, I actually thought it was where King Arthur and Sir Lancelot held their pow-wows. And it was at DOOM that first night that Cutter Hack and I recreated the aura of the Algonquin's legendary Round Table, around which the 3-L Society would gather for long, loud laughter. Cutter was unanimously elected the society chairman.

"Make us laugh" became our rallying cry. The military didn't make that easy. Downtime was not a word in the military lexicon. After all, it was a war, in which everyone had to do his or her job twenty four seven. With little else to do, and few safe places to go, too much downtime was a recipe for trouble. You would either start doing things that you shouldn't do, or go to places where you shouldn't be, which were activities that were very dangerous to oneself and others. So the challenge was to incorporate "entertainment" into everything which we were supposed to do, which we were allowed to do, or which we just did.

To this day, I am still wont to say "Entertain me" when I walk into a room, much to the confusion of people who don't know where I'm coming from. The hootch where we lived, the club where we dined, the gym where we exercised, and the hospital where we worked were the designated military venues to channel our activities. But, as I learned from my vineyard, birds gotta fly and deer gotta eat. Well, humans have to test, have to push the envelope, have to try to get away with something, and have to just be human.

SANITY BY INSANITY

Cutter found a secluded corner of the base at the edge of a rice paddy. He created a driving range at which the officers could compete for prizes. If you hit a drive which detonated a land mine, you got a free steak for dinner that night. Three land mines got you a free bottle of Champagne. The first golfer to achieve one hundred detonations won dinner with the weekly visiting USO troupe. The pretty smiles of the lovely young damsels who sang and danced was the only bright spot in the landscape of that war-torn country.

But as the harsh reality of the earth's turn brings all good things to an end, so too did it wipe away the golfers' smiles in a single stroke. Military surveillance quickly solved the problem of the detonating land mines in the rice paddy, so close to the base. Our group of physicians and dentists was threatened with a court-martial and a dishonorable discharge for dishonorably discharging land mines, for threatening the security of the world, and for being de facto communists. When we heard the threats, we cheered, broke into laughter, and danced like choreographed high-fiving football players in the end zone following a touchdown. The military realized that perception was reality. If it was perceived that you could get yourself out of the quagmire with bad behavior, then the military was going to see a lot of it. Moreover, everyone knew that we were conscientious and doing more than the military ever expected.

All that happened was that the driving range was closed, but shortly after, an emergency meeting of the 3-L Committee was convened to look for a new gig. A makeshift tennis court appeared behind the infirmary. The court surface was a mosaic of black dental rubber dams and silver duct tape, and the net was surgical gauze tied to a pole at each end with dental floss.

Nobody looked more like a tennis player than Deuce Stringer, the Assistant Hospital Administrator. He was tall, muscular, and nimble. Although it sounds like a backhanded compliment, he would have been the spitting image of General George Custer in short pants if only the military would have allowed him to let his golden locks hang to his shoulders. The resemblance was wildly striking, especially because Deuce was always on the wrong side of a tennis massacre, which he attributed to the fact that the sun was always in his eyes. No matter on which side of the net he played, he claimed that the sun adjusted itself to shoot its arrows of blinding light right into his baby blues. Inexplicably, he seemed to have a similar problem when playing tennis on an indoor court. There, he explained, the fluorescent ceiling fixtures would rotate to create a glare wherever he stood or to wherever he ran.

Deuce, a bachelor, had the hots for one of the nurses, Lieutenant Lacey Love. He was sure that they were a perfect match, but his score in getting her to acknowledge him was "Love, Mr. Stringer." Deuce volleyed strategies back and forth in his mind to come up with a way to get Lieutenant Love's attention. He realized that he needed a winning stroke of luck. It came quickly, like a service ace, but landed softly like a lob plopping before him. Lieutenant Love and he were paired as mixed doubles partners in one of the round-robin matches. Nervous, Deuce double faulted, foot faulted, and faulted himself in every way he could. As defeat at the hands of their opponents loomed, Lieutenant Love's dismay spread like dark clouds overhead, providing the shade that Deuce needed to win her over.

Deuce and Lacey became engaged while "in country," to use precise military lingo, and the 3-L Committee scheduled a party at our hootch. Wanting to create a bar to be remembered, a chair was set on top of a table. While Deuce sat in the chair, the orthopedic surgeon, Tennyson Dunn, wrapped Deuce's body in plaster. Tenn, as he was called, placed breathing straws in Deuce's nostrils while the plaster around his face was setting. Then, with breathtaking surgical finesse, he cut the entire cast right down the middle, from the split ends of the hair on Deuce's scalp to the fungus under his toenails. With the dexterity of Rodin, Tenn reassembled the hollow cast, as Deuce watched in awe. Next, Tenn hooked up an IV drip bottle on each side of the plaster sculpture, running IV tubing from the bottles to between the plaster legs. He attached surgical clamps to the tubes and filled one IV bottle with bourbon and the other with vodka. He passed urinalysis cups to all. Releasing a surgical clamp, the drink of choice ran into Tenn's cup. Everyone followed suit, putting a hand between Deuce's plaster legs as their cup runneth over. The roar of a rousing toast to Tenn Dunn, an orthopedic surgeon with whom no one ever had a bone to pick, reverberated over the Air Base like a fighter jet taking off into the wild blue yonder. The nurses fought over who should be the bartender, because they all loved how a plastered Deuce served it up.

MERCIFUL WIND
An explosive tornado of swirling dirt and debris
enveloped the young man, stripping his uniform
from a body left without limbs, with shrapnel
souvenirs embedded deeply in his brain.
Hooked to a respirator, the miracle of medicine
kept him alive so that he could spend the rest of
that life wishing he were dead.
When a merciful wind finally took him away, it left
his medals behind, as well as a mirror for others to
see whom had sent him to the avoidable war.

TOY SOLDIER

He would run down the stairs each Christmas
morning, whooping with joy, to a tree
standing resplendently at attention, surrounded
by piles of perfectly wrapped boxes decorated
with luscious bows and glittering stickers.
He would tear into his gifts with the noise,
power, and efficiency of a chain-saw.
Colored paper would fly as the floor became filled
with soldiers, artillery, trucks, tanks, planes, and ships.
His love of all things military never died.
When he was eighteen, he enlisted to begin
the military career of which he had dreamed.
He was sent to Iraq, and then to Afghanistan.
He was ready. He was proud. There was
nothing he wanted to do more than to serve.
No one believed in the American Dream more
than he. But what he was told, what he expected,
what he saw, and what he was ordered to do
stripped him of his honor and his beliefs.
Broken hearted, he fell into a despair
so deep that he was mentally buried
under a dune of sand in a perpetually
dark and bitter cold desert.
He no longer wears the uniform
of his country. No ribbons, metals,
or insignias embellish his shoulders,
chest, and sleeves. His uniform is
now pajamas.
He is a toy soldier in a sand box.

GREAT MAMA

Martha couldn't see the birthday cake, but she felt the heat of the lighted candles against her face as the cake was placed on the table before her. She blew as hard as she could, unable to see how successful she was. The sound of someone else finishing off the candles went unheard. Valerie, her oldest daughter, took Martha's hand and placed the handle of the cake knife firmly against the palm of Martha's right hand. With Valerie's guidance, Martha made the first cut. She heard the faint clapping of hands and the distant singing of Happy Birthday.

Martha Hampton was 90 years old. She took little joy in the celebration around her, although she was grateful for her family's continued devotion. She hoped this would be her last birthday party. Being unable to see, and barely able to hear, was a steeper slope than she was inclined to climb. She smiled, inwardly, thinking that life's incline was steeper than most people acknowledged. As she took a bite of cake, her eyelids followed the closing motion of her mouth. To the others, it appeared that she was sleeping, but Martha was only deep in her memories, which were always more clear when her eyes were closed.

As she looked back to the beginning, while still contemplating the present, her body quivered in hopelessness about the future. The paths of her life were strewn with family members lost in decades of battle, in faraway places, seeking to build a better world. Her head jerked slightly at the thought of her father lying bloodied and breathless, one of 1,811 fatalities at the Battle of Belleau Wood, in 1918, six years to the day after her birth.

Her eyes opened as Valerie held her arm and walked her from the table to the living room, where she sat in her favorite chair. Her eyes closed once again, only to see another American soldier, her husband Jack, felled and gone forever at Pearl Harbor, shortly after she had blown out the candles on the cake at her 29th birthday party. She started as she felt a hand on her shoulder.

"Hi, Great Mama," she heard her great-grandson Todd say. "Can I get you anything: coffee or tea?"

"No, thank you," she said. "I'm fine."

"Okay, Great Mama, just holler if you need me," Todd said, giving her a kiss on the forehead.

Her eyes, always heavy, seemed so much heavier. She drifted away in a heavy sleep, only to be awakened by another tap on another shoulder.

"Mom, we're leaving," Valerie said. "Come, let me help you with your coat."

The cold blast of air rushed through the open door, and it lightened the heaviness in Martha's eyes. Following Valerie's lead, she reached the car and settled into the back seat, grateful that her son-in-law had turned the heat on a few minutes earlier. As the car turned onto the highway, Martha turned back toward her memories. She thought she heard singing, but what she heard wasn't a song, just the word Hoengsong: a cacophony of terror in 1951 which took her son Thomas away from her on a hilltop in Korea, on the same day she turned 39.

She felt the car stop. Her son-in-law's door slammed shut, as her daughter's hand reached into the open door beside her to help her out of the car. They walked slowly together into the house. Valerie helped her with her coat, and then guided her to her bedroom.

Martha lay on her bed, but now she was wide awake. Her eyes were wide open in the darkness of her room. The only glimmer of light was the crescent moon above her window, which she couldn't see. Her memory took her to Vietnam, where a blinding firefight had left her blackened in the sackcloth of mourning at the loss of her grandson Richard, only days after dousing the glimmer of her birthday candles as she turned 59.

Valerie opened Martha's bedroom door to find her mother still sleeping, her breathing more shallow. She picked up the phone and called Dr. Khalil, who arrived within the hour.

"She appears to be comfortable," he said. "I don't think it will be long now. Please, sit with me. We shall wait together."

Martha was aware that she was not alone; however, she felt like the loneliest woman in the world. Her father had been taken from her; and then her husband, son, and grandson. She wanted to be taken. She had been ready to go for so many years, yet she was still here. She thought she heard the television, off in the distance.

"Yes, it's the news," she realized. "What could be new?," she thought. "It's always the same. Nothing will ever change."

Her breathing slowed. Dr. Khalil nodded to Valerie, as a tear trickled down his face. A newscaster's voice announced that the United States was committing more forces to the war on terror. Martha heard another voice. It sounded faraway.

"Good-bye Great Mama, good-bye. Don't worry, I'll be fine."

HOMECOMING

I still had five months of active duty left when I returned stateside. Rinnce and I were to meet at the hotel in San Francisco. I arrived unshaven, wearing a wrinkled, blue Air Force raincoat and a faded cap. Although I looked quite bedraggled, the lobby was filled with a dignified clientele. I was apprehensive about the reception I might receive. When I had been in Hawaii for a week of R&R with Rinnce, I had been surprised at the reaction of fellow American citizens who, seeing me in uniform, took out their disapproval of the war on me. However, the people in the hotel rose and gave me a standing ovation. Each one came over and shook my hand, welcomed me home, and thanked me for my sacrifice. With wet, blurry eyes and a voice overcome with emotion, I checked in at the reception desk.

"Dr. Toon, we didn't realize that you were in the military and just back from Vietnam. We're so sorry. Please give us a moment to upgrade your room, as well as to reduce your charge. Your wife is already in the originally booked room. Please, go and meet her there. Call us when you are ready. The bellhop will escort you to the new room. Welcome back!"

After a whirlwind reunion, Rinnce and I reunited with my parents. While staying with them, I went to the local barber shop. Upon seeing my uniform, the barber refused to cut my hair. When we left my parent's home, a red light appeared in my rear view mirror shortly after we got on the highway.

"No problem," I told Rinnce. "Once he sees this uniform and learns that I'm just back from 'Nam, he'll just wish me good luck." He must have been related to the barber.

My cousin, Father Jesterius, was living near my new base. We arranged for him to meet us for dinner at our off-base housing.

Within minutes of his arrival, we were disagreeing about everything regarding the war. Our voices rose and he stormed out. We never saw or heard from him again.

SHINGLE AND MINGLE

With the military behind me, a shingle on my door, private practice ahead of me, and a new addition to the family all over me, Rinnce and I, along with our infant daughter Spittella, settled into the wished for life. All my new patients joked that practice makes perfect, but it takes more than practice. You've got to travel the highways of learning by attending continuing education seminars to stay on top of the new and to review and re-enforce the old. The problem isn't having to go; the problem is having to stay. Depending on the lecturer, an all day seminar can be a major test of stamina.

The way I see it, lecturers fall into one of three categories. There are the very knowledgeable and renowned clinicians and researchers who just can't help but put everyone to sleep with their factually and statistically replete presentations served up as a platter of soporific drone. The champion in this category is the famous French oral pathologist, Henri Ennui, who talks at a snail's pace, in which his words go like an escargot. Apparently, he suffers from a type of oral pathology known as "speak-leak," a condition in which words formed in the mind become so diluted by the time they are pronounced that they are all received in an indecipherable, low humming, monotone sound.

Then there are the performers interested in holding you in the palm of their hands, while dazzling you with images and accomplishments that could not possibly be real, but which you believe anyway, until you get back to your office and try to replicate them. The foremost lecturer in this category is Dr. Smoke N. Mirrerz, a guy whom you can't look straight in the eye, as each one is either hidden by a gray haze or so mirrorlike that all you see is yourself.

And, of course, every discipline has the lecturers who bare their souls, showing you poor outcomes, mistakes, and tragic results, one after another. They claim that you learn more by an honest discussion of screw-ups, rather than the razzle-dazzle of picture-perfect accomplishments, achieved only in the mind of a showman. These effusively honest men and women, down-to-earth types like you and me, tug at your heartstrings with their openness, and they call to your highest ideals to share your failures publicly, as the way to find clinical perfection. The problem is that their failures still look better than the successes of most of the attendees at the lecture. After hearing from this type of lecturer, one goes home so depressed for holding such a high self-opinion that self-flagellation is the only recourse. Dr. Mea Culpa is the most prominent lecturer of this genre.

The most convenient way one met the annual continuing education requirement was to attend the local dental society monthly dinner meetings. So, on the first Tuesday of every month, you could find me at Ristorante Balsamico, pen and notebook in hand, collecting clinical pearls of wisdom to add to my necklace of skills.

After each meeting, I would retire to the bar with my colleagues Armando, Marlon, and Dennis. We were always the last to leave. As I was driving home after one of the meetings, I saw the flashing red light of a police car pull into view behind me when I stopped at a traffic light. The officer emerged from his car and leaned into my window.

"Good evening, officer," I said, with a cheery lilt. "Is there a problem?"

"You were zigging and zagging from one lane to another," he said coldly.

"Is that a problem? There is no traffic on the road."

"Where are you going?," he inquired.

"Home, I live about two miles up the road."

"Have you been drinking?"

"Have I been drinking? What kind of question is that? Of course I have been drinking. That's what real dentists do at monthly dental meetings."

"What dental meeting?"

"The one every first Tuesday of the month at Ristorante Balsamico."

"Are you a dentist?"

"I was at the meeting. It was a dental meeting. I was drinking, ergo, I am a dentist."

"Okay Doctor, what is your name?," he asked, curtly.

"Salvatore Spittell Toon, at your service. Call me Spit; everyone does, except my mother who still calls me Salvatore," I said proudly, as I thrust my hand toward him to press the flesh in good will."

"Listen Doc. I want you to drive very carefully home now. I will be following you all the way."

"Oh, that won't be necessary, officer. I'll be fine."

"I'm sure you will, but I'm still going to follow you home," he said, with a smile that looked like one Armando would have made.

I pulled into my driveway, and he pulled in right behind me.

"Thank you, officer; I'm home safely."

"I'll just follow you into your apartment building, just to make sure," he said.

"Okay, well then, here we are," I announced as we walked into the building. "Thank you again."

"Which apartment is yours?, he inquired, as I wondered if he was ever going to leave.

"This one right here," I replied, as I put my hand on the door knob. "Well, goodnight."

"I'll just follow you into your apartment to make sure you're there," he noted.

"Well, I'm in, finally," I stated.

"Please let me see you sit on the sofa," he directed, as he helped me off with my coat.

"Officer, I don't want to be rude, or unappreciative, but don't you think this is enough?"

"You can never be too safe. Is your wife at home?"

"Yes, she's sleeping."

"Can she hear us?"

"No, the bedroom door is closed, and she is a very sound sleeper."

"Good, then let's have a nightcap to toast your safe return home."

"Godleigh Hart is right. There is a God, and he works in mysterious ways," I thought as our glasses clicked.

A TAXING SITUATION

I received a notice from the Tax Department stating that a review of Rinnce's and my joint return indicated that we owed an additional $350 from one of the schools at which she taught while I was in Vietnam. As I couldn't find any error, I asked Armando, Marlon, and Dennis to recommend a CPA.

"Got just the guy for you," each one said. "My friend Bob just opened an office. He's a tax attorney and an accountant."

"He might think I'm small potatoes," I replied with concern.

"No, he's a regular guy, and he needs the business," each of them assured me.

"Call me Spit. May I call you Bob?," I asked, upon entering Bob's office, which was small, dark, and dingy."

"No, my name is Robert, pronounced in the French manner."

"Okay, Row-bare it is. Listen, I think the Tax Department is mistaken. I honestly believe that I do not owe them more money."

"Whether you do, or whether you don't, we'll fight them hard and win."

"Bob, I mean Row-bare, I'm not looking for a war here. It sounds like I'll end up owing you more for your services than I owe them."

"Nonsense, we're talking about fairness, justice, and most importantly, victory. It would be sinful to pay the government money to which it was not entitled."

"Row-bare, do I owe them the money or not?"

"We'll find out soon enough."

"Well, don't you know now?," I asked, perplexed.

"One never can be sure, "Robert stated, in a lawyerly sort of way."

"Maybe I should just pay it. How much do I owe you?"

"Relax, my good friend. Let me handle this," Robert stated with amazing confidence.

After several months, Robert, giddy with excitement, called to tell me that I had won my appeal, and that the Tax Department had apologized for its mistake.

I was not at all surprised to receive Robert's bill for $500 to save $350. I had not forgotten his passionate words: "Nonsense, we're talking about fairness, justice, and, most importantly, victory. It would be sinful to pay the government money to which it was not entitled."

Several years later, and no longer living near Robert's office, I received a letter from the Tax Department, for which I called Robert for advice.

"Hi Bob, I mean Row-bare, the Tax Department wants me, or my representative, to meet with them for an audit in their offices up here. Can you handle this from down there?"

"Absolutely, mon ami, just write to them and request that they transfer your records from their office up there to their office down here, where I can represent and handle everything for you."

"Will that be a problem?"

"No, it's very common,"

"Anything to worry about?"

"Probably not. Usually in the transfer of records to another office, everything gets lost, and we never hear about it again."

He was right and, not surprisingly, his bill for the transfer advice was higher than the amount in question for the audit. I felt like I was spitting in the wind.

EXPRESS LINE

Feeling guilty that I had invited friends for dinner at the last minute, I told Rinnce that I would run to the supermarket to pick up what we needed.

"It will take you too long. You're the kind of person who has to walk up and down each aisle, even if you only need one item. I'll go; it will be much more efficient."

"I'll be fine," I reassured her.

True to my claim, I got what I needed quickly, so I pushed my cart up to a checkout line, but behind several overflowing carts. A manager approached me and told me to go through the express line.

"I have too many items for express," I told him.

"It's fine. Don't worry," he said.

"Will you defend me if I come under attack?"

"Sir, it's fine. Don't worry," he repeated.

"The manager sent me here, even though I have too many items," I explained to the express cashier.

"Yeah, yeah, yeah," she muttered, as she started to ring me up. "Are these Bosc or Bartlett pears?" she asked.

"I have no idea," I answered.

"I can't ring you up without a code," she said, as two customers, each carrying one item, lined up behind me.

"Ring these people up first," I offered, graciously.

"I can't, I've already started you."

"Call the pear whatever you want," I suggested.

"I might call it by the wrong name."

"It's okay, it won't hear you, and therefore it will not be offended," I replied.

"I might charge too much, plus skew the inventory," she advised, with a look of dismay at my cavalier attitude.

"Hey, you've got too many items. Get out of the line," the woman behind me blurted out loudly.

"Yes, I know, but the manager sent me here," I emphasized.

"He was wrong. Get out of the line."

"Yeah, what are you doing in this line," a guy holding a six pack of beer yelled.

"See what you've caused," the cashier growled..

"What I've caused?," I barked. "Just ring this stuff up, so I can get out of here."

"What's the problem?," a different manager asked, as he approached quickly.

"This guy isn't supposed to be here."

"Sir, step aside," the manager said, taking my arm.

"No," I shouted. "Another manager told me to come here. You people don't know what you're doing."

"You people?," the manager said, glaring.

"You people?," the cashier said, scowling.

"You people?," everyone in line shouted.

"Yes, you people," I shouted back, as I started to pick up each item, one by one, from my cart and hand it to the cashier. "This is a Forelle pear; ring it up. This is a Macintosh apple; ring it up. This is endive;

ring it up. The Latin name for this plant is 'Leafusupyourassius'; ring it up."

"Sir," the plant is an Aspidistra," a woman in the adjacent check-out lane cried out to me. "Would you like me to tell the cashier what you would like her to do with it?"

I waved to her appreciatively as I was dragged out of the store.

CLUTCH

Right at the peak of rush hour, my new car broke down in the tunnel. Single-handedly, I brought a city to its knees, something I wanted to do to my car dealer, Clutch Wheeler.

Clutch was like a member of the family. He had been my parents' car dealer for 40 years. Clutch specializes in people like me, who have absolutely no interest, whatsoever, in automobiles. For me, the only requirement for a car is that it be reliable, and as usual, Clutch had let me down. I consider a car to be no more than a box with four wheels and a motor. I don't care what brand insignia adorns the grille, what color covers its surface, or if it has any bells and whistles. Whenever it needs to be serviced, Clutch picks it up, loans me a car, and returns it.

Whenever I need a new car, Clutch asks me what I want, but sells me whatever he has, which is never what I selected..

"Spit, I think it's time that you replace the car. It has served you well. I think we should leave it on the tow truck and let them tow it to the junk yard in the sky," he said, looking at me sadly.

"Whatever, Clutch; you're the boss, but first check with 'the Big Molar in the Sky' to see if he or she wants it for someone else."

"Spit, trust me, 'the Big Molar in the Sky' wouldn't even give your car to the Devil."

"Okay, Clutch, get me a new one. Don't ask me what I want, or what color I prefer, because I know that you will come up with something else, but that's fine."

And that's exactly what he did: he came up with something else. Don't ask, they all look the same to me, but I did recognize my old car being driven around town, like all my other cars, by a little old lady that "the Big Molar in the Sky wouldn't even give to the Devil."

Later that week, Rinnce and I drove to a dinner party in our new car. In the middle of dinner, the door bell rang, and in walked Dr. Kingsley Kidd, a local pediatrician who lived across the street from our hosts.

"Oh, please forgive me," he whined, while rubbing his hands and sweating profusely, "but I just backed into a Grande Turbo Charger Coupe LX395. I am so, so sorry. I will pay for all damages."

Nobody reacted.

"Hello out there! Who here owns a Grande Turbo Coupe LX395?," our gracious and affable hostess said, looking around the table at each guest as she awaited an answer which never came.

"It's a black and silver car with license plate number GHA7498," Kingsley added.

"What color did you say?," I asked, jumping up.

"Black and silver."

"Does it look new?," I asked.

"Not anymore," he whimpered.

"So, you will just pay for the repairs, personally?," I asked, seeking reassurance.

"Yes, use my dealer, Clutch Wheeler. Tell him to bill me directly."

"Great, he's my dealer too."

I called Clutch the next day, and he said that he would take care of everything. Two days later, I received a phone call from Dr. Kidd's insurance agent who was outraged by the arrangement.

"Look, Mr. Proteccione," I stated firmly, "your client instructed me to deal directly with Clutch Wheeler. Don't bother me. Work it out with your client and Clutch."

"What the hell is going on, Clutch," I said over the phone. "Why is this bozo blocking his client's wishes?"

"He doesn't want the word to get around that his clients would rather pay on their own so they can avoid his bullshit."

Mr. Proteccione continued to call me, accusing me of engineering a conspiracy against him. I took great pleasure one day in telling him *en français* to "*Va te faire foutre*," before hanging up.

Several months later, at another dinner party, I found myself sitting beside an insurance agent named Patrick Proteccione. He tried to make small talk with me, but I kept avoiding him, a tricky thing to do when you're sitting right next to the guy. He kept asking my name, to which I would garble "Spit" inarticulately. A few minutes later, he made a sudden turn toward me, his right eye raised, and his finger in my face.

"I know who you are," he said, with so much disdain that it drooled out of both corners of his mouth.

"I think you have me confused with someone else," I said.

"No, no, no; you hung up on me, as you shouted something in a foreign language."

"How could I have done that?," I asked. "I am not versed in a foreign tongue. I took four years of Latin in high school. I never could speak it, no less shout it."

"How dare you do that to me. You were trying to take advantage of my client. You are a sleazeball, Toon. Who the hell invited you to this party?"

"Oh, I wasn't invited. I crashed the party, just like your client crashed into me."

He pushed his chair back from the table, stood up, threw down his napkin, and stormed out of the dining room. The hostess rushed after him, calling out "Patrick, Patrick, don't go." When she returned, her dagger looks were penetrating deeply into my flesh and soul.

"Spit, you are such a pain in the ass. Why did you insult poor Patrick?"

"I didn't insult him," I said. "He was coming on to me, and I asked him to provide full, no-deductible protection, just to be safe."

"It was supermarket déjà vu all over again.

PETER PAN

"I'll meet you at the workshop," Rinnce stated, as I tagged along dutifully at the conference to which she had dragged me. You can check out the display tables until then."

"It takes a special man to do what you are doing," a woman beside me observed, as I took a seat in the workshop room.

"And why is that?" I asked.

"Not only are you the only male in this workshop, the rumor is that you are the only male at the conference."

"Really?," I responded, as I looked around the room.

"Never fear, sir, we are all harmless."

"I never doubted it," I answered.

All the women in the room were talking loudly and with great animation about womanly things, while awaiting the start of the formal workshop program.

"Oh sir," one of the ladies called out.

"Are you speaking to me?," I asked, as I looked over my shoulder at a bevy of womanly grins and twinkling eyes.

"As you are the only sir in the room, and the whole conference as well, the answer to your query is yes. My friends and I were just discussing our belief that men go through life singing along with Peter Pan that they don't want to grow up. Do you sing that song?"

I rose slowly from my chair and turned to address the ladies whom I felt were enjoying this nonsense a wee bit too much at my expense. Pausing to heighten the theatricality sparking in the air, I looked squarely at my interrogator and pointed my index finger straight at her.

"No man has, or ever will, grow up," I stated. "It is the blessing of being male, the superior gender. Accept it, embrace it, deal with it, and get over it. Pray that if there is such a thing as reincarnation, you will return as a male."

Bedlam broke out. The woman became a launched missile crashing into my midsection and taking me down with a ferociousness only reserved for preventing a running back from crossing the goal line. Every woman in the room piled on, except one, who finally blew a whistle. She offered her hand and pulled me up for all to see the frilly pink dress in which I was covered.

"We girls think that you will be safer dressed like this for the rest of the conference," my nemesis said, as the other women danced about like a victorious football team.

"No, I really don't think that's the right outfit for tonight. It's just not you," Rinnce said, as she walked into the workshop. "It certainly is very chic, but it makes you look fat."

CLOWNING AROUND

As anyone who knows me will tell you, whenever I walk into a room, I skip the usual and customary salutations and just say "Entertain me."

I always wonder whether people are laughing with me or at me. It is a natural thing for me to do, because I am always trying to get a laugh by humorously playing off what I hear, or purposely setting someone up for some hopefully amusing follow-up repartee.

People who don't know me, don't get me. People who do know me, get me, have heard it all before, and have had enough of me. This leaves me a bit defensive, until someone laughs at something I've said. Others will then jump in with alarm at the sound of laughter to admonish the person who has laughed to cease and desist, because it only encourages me. And this is why I am never sure if the sound of laughter is with me or at me. But that's okay, because I know who I am and why I do what I do. Down deep, I really do know who laughs with me and who laughs at me, but it doesn't matter, because I just need to laugh, even if it's by myself, at myself.

My wife is always giving me her signature gaze when I get rolling, and when we're alone later, she'll give me a mouthful of criticism about how I push the envelope "much too far, much too far."

"Exhausting" seems to be the answer most people give to describe my persona. I call myself a social provocateur, or the devil's advocate, who breaks the silent, insipid, and vapid ice jams of social interaction. But then again, horse's ass is not an unheard alternative assessment that has been offered.

In any case, I try to get beyond whether the laughter is pro or con. I try to tell myself that it doesn't matter, because I consider myself self-deprecating, although the accusations of being irritating do have merit. But for me, a world without repartee about sex, sports, politics, and religion is beyond boring. "Nice day, isn't it?" doesn't get the juices flowing for me, just as conversations about automotive accessories don't start my engine.

Sometimes, when my wife is really piling it on about my nonsense, I will quote, all evening at a party, Eliza Doolittle from the musical *My Fair Lady* : "How nice of you to have me come; the rain in Spain falls mainly on the plain; and hurricanes hardly happen in Hartford, Hereford, and Hampshire." This, of course, engenders a critical barrage from my wife about my being disengaged, rude, not myself, boring, and socially unacceptable.

So, if we ever cross paths, don't worry if you don't laugh at my nonsense. I'll laugh for you.

PORTRAIT

A colorful portrait without
a frame hung starkly
against an eggshell white wall.
The eyes of the man on the canvas
magnetically drew me in, and
slowly I walked closer to him.
He was a man of years who
showed his time, with a face
unshaven for days. Accompanying
his frown and worn down look
were two eyes filled with sadness.
A black derby, with an orange
ribbon, rested atop his head, and
a red scarf surrounded his neck
while it sprawled over one shoulder.
His shirt was tattered cloth garishly
colored like an artist's rag, and
his lips were painted white.
A twisted, bumpy nose was covered
in a greasepaint of bloody red,
while green and black surrounded
his eyes, and his cheeks were hued
in yellow and red.
I stood, as he hung, and
we stared at each other
in a silent stillness of wonder,
but I could not hold my
breath for long, and when
I let it go, it fogged the
mirror into which I looked,
and the sad clown went away.

DOUBLE VISION

No shine or sheen was seen
reflected from the mirrored
silver glass, only refracted,
doubled disreflection and
disrespection, filtered by a
cataract cloud into discolored
tints of appalling pallor and
disbelieving cries of denial.
"Who? Not me!"
"Become my father?"
"Never!"
A wink and a smile was
inevitability exchanged, while
my father seemed as surprised
to see me, as I was to see him.

SEARCH

Alone in a bar, I tread
water in a bottle of wine,
savoring its petulant
petillance which tickled
my skin.
I stared into each bubble
in search of an answer,
but before I could find it
in the clear crystal shell,
it burst.
Then a singular bubble of
larger size rose from the
sediment to the ullage above,
where it began to babble
to me about things I didn't
want to hear.
The tickle of the petillance
waned, and I ordered another
bottle of wine, but this time
non-sparkling.

CINEMA

On a palette of swirling black, white,
and gray images, a parade of actors
and actresses march and carry me
off to a former time.
Some I see for the first time; others I
have seen in the twilight of their careers.
Yet, there is a comforting familiarity about
them all.
These are the stars on whom the eyes
of my parents shined. It was about them
and the characters they played that my
parents spoke with an affinity filled with
excitement and appreciation. I see my
mother, happy and animated, as she
recreates her evening out for me.
I know that I immerse myself in these old
films, not for how much I enjoy them in
their own right, but for the memories
they stir of my parents, which help
me appreciate the influence they had
on my life: my thinking, my mannerisms,
and my regrets.
These swirling black, white, and gray
images of early Hollywood are my
personal Rorschach inkblot test.

EXACTLY!

"And how do you feel about that?," Lyon Couch, my therapist and good friend, asked as he had so many times before.

"That? Which that? I'm frustrated with this tiresome psychiatric schtick of asking how I feel about what you refer to as 'that.' About which feeling, exactly, do you want to know how I feel?"

"The same one I'm feeling about you?"

"I can't know what you're feeling unless you tell me," I snapped.

"Exactly," Lyon exclaimed.

"Sorry, buddy," I replied. "You, of all people, know that I have a phobia about letting certain things hang out."

"Spit, you're like a split infinitive. You like to put a word in the wrong place to obfuscate, rather than clarify, your real feeling."

"I hate it when you use dirty words like obfuscate with me," I confessed.

"Exactly! There you go again trying to nudge the conversation in another direction to avoid revealing a feeling."

"Are you and Novella Nottingham working as a tag team against me?"

"Spit, Novella is not real; I am."

"Don't delude yourself, Lyon. And, of all people, you know that I am more interested in authenticity than reality."

"Yes, as in your fondness for the player piano metaphor."

"Exactly!"

"So, correct me if I'm wrong, but you believe that a lip-synching piano player at a player piano captures the essence of life more powerfully than Sisyphus."

"Exactly! The piano player speaks no words and plays no music. He or she fakes it. It's illusion. We're all faking it, acting out on Shakespeare's world stage. We are emperors without clothes. Every time a plastic surgeon, or a cosmetic dentist, caters to a patient's vanity, we all lose a layer of authenticity. Implants, injections, nips, tucks, lifts, augmentations, reductions, orthodontics, and dental laminate veneers transform authentic realities, oxymoronically, into false realities. Moreover, if the lip-synching piano player at the player piano is doing his gig at a place called 'Chez Sisyphus,' maybe it's a synergistic double metaphor of serendipity. We have man fated to eternal entrapment; futilely, authentically, and endlessly pushing, by individual sheer force, a large boulder up a mountain while listening to ersatz canned music from a player piano with a lip-synching pianist."

"Whoa baby, Spit. Even for a dentist, that's quite a mouthful. It's time for a drink."

Lyon opened the small refrigerator under his desk, took out a small bottle of Prosecco, poured half into one glass, and half into another. We raised our glasses and lip-synched "Rock and Roll forever."

CONFLUENCE

I was sitting at the far end of the bar reviewing our wine list. A man, about my age, entered the saloon, walked to the far end of the bar, pulled up a stool, and ordered a drink. He and our bartender, Schottzy Glass, engaged in some conversation during which Schottzy directed him to me.

"The bartender said you wouldn't mind if I interrupted you about a matter I am investigating," he said as he approached.

"Not at all. Call me Spit; everyone does, except my mother, who still calls me Salvatore."

"Call me Hoot; everyone does, except my mother, who still calls me Harvey," he said, as he stretched out a hand and flashed a smile that a dentist needed to remake.

"How can I help you?" I asked, wondering what he was investigating

"I'm Hellman — a hell of a last name, I know. I've always wished it was Heavenman. No, I'm not a cleric, far from it. Actually, I'm a dick, in the private eye sense of the word. So, I suppose my name fits. I've been dicking around, so to speak, for longer than I like to admit. Yeah, no way to deny it, I'm slowing down: shorter in the step, blurrier in the stare, and sputtering in the speech. For the first time, I'm saying that retirement seems plausible. I never thought that I would hear words like that coming from my mouth, because I've always believed that a man's work defines him as a person. The marquis on "Retirement Theater" has always been blank for me, but I'm beginning to think that some of the coming attractions might be fun: a little golf, some travel, and a bachelor pad on the beach. No, I'm not married. I lost my wife a long time ago. P.I. isn't the same turn on for the fair sex as M.D., D.M.D., M.B.A., C.P.A., or J.D. But I'm still around and slogging away, but it gets harder every day.

"I know, I know. I don't look like your picture of a private eye. Years ago, I probably was picture perfect, but the Vietnam jungle, as well as the one out there about which everyone talks, takes its toll. Yeah, I've passed through my share of toll booths in my life, and I've tossed a lot of my soul, in loose change, into those baskets.

"I just take odd jobs now and then, as a favor for a friend, or for someone about whom I feel sorry. And that is why I am here. A lawyer friend of mine asked me to help him reconnect an adopted person with her biological family."

"And where do I fit in?," I asked politely.

"My client discovered information about her adoption, an event about which she had never been told, in going through family records after her parents died. With the natural urge to know about her biological family, she began the search, but the bureaucracy was convoluted, immobile, and uncaring. The best it could offer was an ever quickening treadmill of referrals to different offices, all leading back to from where she started, more frustrated than before. She consulted with her attorney who asked me to help her. Checking with my contacts in Social Services, I was able to slide through the hallways of red taped wallpaper, to unseal sealed records, and to identify the names of her biological parents. I keep searching for people with whom there is a middle or last name match. I'm looking for a cousin whose middle name might be Brush and/or whose maiden name might be Wehl, spelled *W-e-h-l*."

"Well, Hoot, you're either very lucky or very good. My wife is the former Rinnce Brush Wehl."

"Does she look anything like this?," he asked, as he pulled a photo out of the inner breast pocket of his sport jacket. "I take that for an affirmative," he added, as he saw my draw drop to the floor.

"Hoot, please join me in that booth in the corner. I will join you there with Rinnce, momentarily." I bounded up the stairs to our office, where Rinnce sat at a desk tabulating the receipts from the night before. "Play with me on this," I pleaded. "Don't ask me questions. Follow me downstairs. You're going to have a hoot when you hear what our guest downstairs is going to tell you."

After introducing her to Hoot, I watched her closely as the story unfolded. When Hoot handed her the photo, her jaw dropped as much as mine had. She peppered Hoot with a machine gun spray of questions, being in the middle of the next question before Hoot had finished answering the previous one. When the dust settled, we all decided to meet again the following day for lunch in the very same booth.

Hoot arrived promptly with Rinnce's cousin on his arm. The two women ran toward each other and fell into a mutual embrace filled with tears. I knew we wouldn't be eating anything very soon. We learned that Rinnce's maternal aunt had an affair with a married man with whom she became pregnant. The two decided to give the baby up for adoption. Subsequently, Rinnce's aunt and the man with whom she had the affair got married. However, Rinnce's cousin, Alicia, was now in a new, unknown, parallel, and inaccessible world about which no one was ever told. Ironically, that world was just a few miles down the road from Rinnce's house, and even if they would have ever crossed paths, neither would have suspected anything.

On that day, Rinnce not only found a cousin, but I found a best friend: a guy named Harvey, whom everyone called Hoot. We named the booth at the saloon, in which this all happened, "Hellman's Booth," where Hoot now spends most of his time holding court.

ÉCHANGE CULTUREL

"I think a French family is moving into the house next door," Rinnce announced, as she looked out our kitchen window.

"How do you know they are French?," I asked smugly.

"The woman is wearing a mink coat and carrying a poodle," she said.

"Well, that makes it a certainty," I agreed, with enough sarcasm to flush clean the sewers of Paris.

Rinnce dragged me over to offer our new neighbors a hearty American welcome and a gracious French *bienvenue*. A woman partially opened the door, peering through the narrowly created slit with a tentative look.

"*Bonjour, Je m'appelle Monique. Je regrette, mais je ne parle pas anglais bien*," our new neighbor said.

Rinnce turned to me with one of those silent, but aggressive, bragging looks, filled with enough self-satisfaction to make any man fear that he might lose a part of his body which he held especially dear.

Rinnce and I became great friends with Monique and her husband Raoul. One Sunday, Raoul invited me to share *un digestif*. We sat across from one another at the coffee table in the living room. A bottle of brandy was placed next to two diminutive glasses. A small dish on the table contained a few tiny olives, which stared up at me with such sad eyes that I almost believed that they were silently pleading for cardiopulmonary resuscitation. Raoul poured *des gouttes* into my brandy glass. It wasn't hard to figure out that *gouttes* meant drops. I held the glass upside down over my mouth and squeezed it for a full minute before any liquid hit my tongue.

"You know, Speet," Raoul said, as I was preparing to leave a few hours later, *en France*, a bottle of *Armagnac*, *comme ça*, would last for many months, if not years. We, no you, drank the whole bottle in three hours. *C'est merveilleux*."

"I have to get some of that stuff," I said, stumbling over a tongue that seemed thicker than usual. And I did, but none was as good as that first bottle, on that one Sunday afternoon, with Raoul.

Having developed a working knowledge of French in my years at Hinterland College, I hoped that our new neighbors would help me to perfect my fluency. Raoul and I agreed to *un échange culturel* in which we would teach each other slang, vernacular, idioms, and dirty words. Monique said that she could teach me everything I needed to know, if I agreed to a full week's immersion *dans le boudoir* with her. Rinnce gave me that same look that she had given me at Monique's front door. I figured that I'd better stick with Raoul's offer.

Raoul and Monique came for dinner one evening. I knew from previous social engagements with them that they liked to drink Screwdrivers.

"*Voudriez vous un tournevis*," I asked proudly, having looked up how to say screwdriver *en français*.

"Why would we want a screwdriver?" Raoul asked.

"I thought you liked Screwdrivers," I said.

"What is there to like?,"

"Well, they are refreshing."

"How can a screwdriver be refreshing?," he asked, confused.

"Well, because we put a lot of ice in the glass."

"Why would you put a screwdriver in a glass and pour ice on top of it?"

"Am I not pronouncing the word correctly?"

"*Oui*, it is that tool you twist to put a screw in place."

"Uh, Raoul, we call vodka and orange juice a Screwdriver, don't you?"

"Non."

"What do you call vodka and orange juice?," I asked, meekly.

"We call it vodka *et jus d'orange*," he said. "What else would we call it?"

"Well, now you know what we thought you called it."

"You Americans try too hard. Do you know the expression *que sera sera*?"

"Oui, Raoul, I do, but as part of our échange culturel, let me teach you this one: I screwed up."

"Speet, as we are in the échange culturel mode, I want to ask you a question."

"*C'est d'accord*, buddy. Let's keep the échange culturel rolling. Shoot."

"Shoot? Why? I have no gun."

"It's slang for bring it on."

"Was I supposed to bring something more than a bottle of Armangnac?"

"No, I just meant that you should continue."

"Oh yes, you Americans make everything much too complicated. My question is about a word everyone at work uses all the time. It seems to be used in many ways. Sometimes it seems to be a verb. Other times it sounds like an adjective. Sometimes people use it when they're mad. Other times they say it laughing. I am embarrassed to ask what it means. It's not in my dictionary. Monique doesn't know the word either."

"*Qu'est-que c'est le mot*?," I asked, trying to improve my French accent.

"I think it is spelled *p-h-u-q-u-e*," he replied. "It rhymes with book."

"Are you fucking kidding me, Raoul?" I asked in disbelief, as I burst into laughter.

"Yes. No. I mean yes, that is the word. They say it in different forms: phuque, phuqued, phuquing, and phuquer."

"Raoul, it's not fook; it's fuck, and it's spelled *f-u-c-k*. Generally, it refers to sexual intercourse, but in everyday speech, it is used for emphasis; to make a point, or to make a feeling stronger."

"How about that," he said. "I teach you about Armagnac, and all you do is teach me about this fucking word. It's not fucking fair. What a screwy situation."

"A few more gouttes of tournevis?," I asked, as I saw that his glass was empty.

UNITED NATIONS

"Reence, I would like to take English lessons with you," Monique announced one day. "Raoul's company will pay for them."

"Monique, you don't have to pay me for lessons. I will be learning French, at the same time, from you." Rinnce replied.

"I won't be paying; the company will."

"Well, I won't accept any money. It has to be free between you and me."

Monique agreed, reluctantly, but she began to refer other French assignees to Rinnce for lessons, from whom Rinnce did accept whatever the company paid. Soon, assignees from different countries began to call, and in a matter of months our house began to look like the United Nations.

The corporate assignments were anywhere from one to three years in length; however, many of the assignees returned for subsequent assignments, or returned for a meeting, or would just be en route to somewhere else. To this day, Rinnce still gets calls and e-mails from her former students: husband, wife, or child. And, of course, if and when they're in town, she invites them for dinner.

We, too, received many invitations to dine at the homes of the assignees. Over the years, Rinnce and I were exposed to an international sampling of dishes, the names of which we had never heard, like the Brazilian dish *feijoada*, a stew like dish similar to the French *cassoulet*, *pot au feu*, and *bouillabaisse*. Well, not exactly like them, but you get the idea. We were transformed from old fashioned, American meat and potatoes, provincial eaters into adventurous, world class, gourmet, dining aficionados.

Well, not exactly. We were at a dinner party at the home of one of Rinnce's Japanese students, Hiroshi, who liked to say "Call me Harry." He passed me a plate of small fish, very cute small fish with sad looking eyes and a diminutive tail. I wondered how one trimmed such an offering to make it suitable to eat. I watched in horror as he popped the cute little creatures head first into his mouth like popcorn, sometimes chomping down before the tail had made it past his lips.

It was imperative that I make an instant culinary decision, and I made it. With a fish in hand, I passed it across my mouth, and then lowered it to my sport coat pocket, where I would discreetly drop the fish as I lip-synched the act of fish chewing. Hiroshi, the perfect host, kept offering me more, delighted with my apparent love for this sacred treat. When I got home, a pack of stray cats picked up my scent before I could open the front door. Rinnce had to call an ambulance. My sport coat required 72 stitches.

WANDERLUST

The adventures that Rinnce's corporate assignees experienced, in a new land and in a new language, stirred up our juices to try the same. Travel brochures began to lay scattered on the tables of our lives. I also began to look for international opportunities for American dentists. During a lunch break in my dental office, I came upon a full page ad in the back of one of my dental journals for Gusher Oil.

"We suck, but only for oil, all over the world," the ad proclaimed proudly.

The company was looking for dentists to care for their employees and families overseas. I didn't see Paris, Rome, Stockholm, or Vienna on the list of their locations: cities that were on our short list of places to which we would have considered going. Gusher was looking for dentists to go to Hahakabia. Well, thinking "ha ha" to that, and having no intention whatsoever of even considering such an assignment, I still filled out the attached postcard for more information, put it in the mail, and then forgot about it.

Six months later, as I was trying to tackle an impacted wisdom tooth on the quarterback for the high school football team, my dental assistant, Saliva Godiva, told me that I had a phone call from Texas. Since the wisdom tooth was having more success in tackling me, I told Saliva to take a message as I assumed that the call was from a dental insurance company for one of our local employers. It was, in fact, Gusher Oil's Corporate Offices in Houston. I was surprised that after six months they were calling for an interview, when all I had asked for was an information packet, which I never received. I didn't return the call.

Every day for two weeks, a woman named Cougar Lugar called me from Gusher Oil. Each time that I spoke with her, I indicated that I had no interest in going to Hahakabia, and that it would be dishonest of me to lead her on. She kept urging me to come for the interview, emphasizing that there would be no obligation, and assuring me that I would like what I saw and heard.

After two weeks of hard lobbying, Cougar had her teeth deep in my throat and dragged Rinnce and me to Gusher's corporate headquarters. In our walk from the hotel to the Gusher Oil Building, we found ourselves in a parade of hundreds of other people who were there for interviews: engineers, geologists, accountants, teachers, nurses, dentists, and physicians. The morning was spent watching promotional videos and listening to orientation information. It was crystal clear that Hahakabia didn't have the bistros, brasseries, tapas bars, cabarets, cinemas, and theater schedule for which we were looking overseas.

We were sent to lunch to meet with our professional liaison, Dr. Upton Nez, the chief dentist at Gusher Oil in Hahakabia. Although he was American, he acted like he was an emir of considerable influence. There were several other dentists at the round table, all sycophants jockeying for his attention. Rinnce and I sat in silence, not knowing whether to laugh or to vomit.

"Aren't you going to engage this high dental mucky-muck from Hahakabia?," she asked.

"No," I answered. "We've come at their insistence, and we've been assured that there is no obligation."

After lunch, we had individual interviews with Dr. Nez. It was already three o'clock and we had not yet checked out of the hotel. As our flight was in two hours, I knew time was getting short to get our luggage and to catch the plane. I sat politely in the interview as "Mucky" tried to dazzle us with his charm and importance, but I made no effort to win him over. I suddenly bolted up, shook his hand, and told him how much I appreciated his time, but that we had to rush to check out of the hotel so that we wouldn't miss our flight. We barely made it. Rinnce berated me, again, for being disengaged and rude.

"Do you want to go to Hahakabia," I asked, knowing that I had asked her the same question many times before.

"Of course not," she said. "Do you think I'm crazy?"

I was back at my dental chair to resume playing tackle dentistry with impacted wisdom teeth. On the third day back, Cougar Lugar was on the phone and all over the field in lockstep with every move I made.

"Congratulations, Dr. Toon. Dr. Nez has notified us that you are his first choice for the job in Hahakabia."

"That can't possibly be true," I said. "I sat through lunch and the interview like a blob. I rudely and prematurely terminated the interview. There is no way in hell that I am his first selection. Even if everyone else declined an offer, he still wouldn't offer it to me."

"He did, and he wants you in Hahakabia next week to see the operation. He hopes that you will accept his offer."

"Cougar, listen to me. Something is whacko here. I'm not interested," I told her as convincingly as I could.

She called me every day for two more weeks. Each time, I stood my ground, emphasizing that even if I was interested, my wife and daughter would have to go with me and agree to live there. Cougar kept upping the ante, telling me that I could have whatever I wanted and whatever I needed, with no obligation.

"Dr. Toon, I will make a bet with you," she said.

Although I like bets, as Novella Nottingham will attest, Cougar's challenge made me uneasy.

"The terms being what?," I asked.

"I bet that you will like what you see and that you will accept the job, but if you don't, we will not think poorly of you. We will not pressure you, and we will just pay you for your time. That's it: no ifs, ands, or buts. You can't lose."

She had worn me down. We made arrangements to leave our daughter Spittella with friends, having decided that it was crazy to take her with us. We then headed off to Hahakabia, wondering why we were doing such a crazy thing. I knew that I would need to see Lyon Couch many times upon our return.

We landed in the kingdom early in the morning, tired and irritable. Mucky was there waiting for us in traditional Arabic garb, astride a camel, and attended by several aides also on camels. He gave us our robes and head covers. My head cover, which was called a *keffiyeh,* looked like a red and white checkered tablecloth from our favorite Italian trattoria. Boosting us onto our camels, he led us to a temporary, tented compound where we would be based. Once settled, he boosted us, again, onto our camels, and with a man from Terorara named Mohammed, who was to be our personal assistant, we began our tour.

Before we were taken to the clinical facilities, Mucky took us to the residential tents of several of the other staff members with whom I would be working. At each tent there were two stills, each of which produced an alcoholic drink: "Brown" or "White." The "Brown" was like whiskey; the "White" was like vodka. At each tent, we were offered a glass of each to sample. It seemed that we were lucky enough to be there just in time for the annual "Brown" and "White" competition, an event which everyone took very seriously. We feigned delight that we would still be there when the winners were announced. The alcohol was very strong; I was tired and hungry; and I got somewhat inebriated. The day went on forever. It seemed that all anyone did was make and drink "Brown" and "White." Despite being under the influence of the Arabic brew, I was still alert enough to recognize that Mucky had a puzzled look every time I spoke. I asked if there was something bothering him.

"Yes, you do not seem like the very quiet person whom I met in Houston. You have very strong opinions, and you are very much an extrovert," he said, clearly signaling that this was a problem for him.

The last person we met that day was Dr. Wayne Johnson, a good old cowboy from Wyoming, who had been working side by side with the effete, pompous Dr. Nez in the dental clinic for the past 13 years. Wayne and I hit it off right away, as did Rinnce and his wife. Though my head was spinning and Mucky's face was blurry, his displeasure was clearly visible.

That evening, Mucky had a welcoming party for us. Everyone was very friendly, and Rinnce and I had a wonderful time. The next morning at the dental clinic Mucky ignored me, and he never spoke to me again. Wayne, however, took me under his wing. At dinner with him and his wife, we learned that he and Mucky had disliked each other from day one. I concluded that Mucky had assumed that I was a nerdy, dorky, geeky, malleable blob, whom he could mold into an ally against the strong willed, buzz saw personality of his lone dentist partner. I began to plan on how we could get on an earlier plane out of Hahakabia.

Wayne told me not to worry about the tense relations he had with Mucky. He introduced me to his Swiss banking representative to learn how to set up a secret account, because "I would need it for all the money I would be making as a consultant for the contractors."

"What contractors?," I asked.

"The ones building all the apartment buildings in town."

"Wayne, I'm a dentist. I never got my Home Repairs Merit Badge in Boy Scouts, and I don't know anything about constructing apartment buildings," I said in astonishment

"Sure you do; you'll see," he assured me.

The next day, he took me to the construction site. A man came running up to us. He shook Wayne's hand enthusiastically, while telling him how glad he was to see him.

"Dr. Wayne, my good friend, I'm glad that you are here. I need you to tell me if the bathroom which I just had wallpapered is okay."

"Mohammed, I want you to meet my very good friend, Dr. Toon. You can call him Spit; everyone does, except his mother, who still calls him Salvatore. He will be working with me, and he will inspect the bathroom," Wayne explained confidently.

"Okay, Dr. Wayne. I'm a little uncomfortable not having you look, but if you say Dr. Toon, I mean Dr. 'Speet,' is your friend, then he is my friend."

I followed Mohammed to the third floor via an unfinished stairway. He led me to the bathroom in question. It was too small for both of us to stand in it together, for which I was grateful.

"So, Dr. Speet, what do you think? Is it a good job? It cost me close to ten thousand dollars to wallpaper just this one bathroom."

I looked at one piece of wallpaper rising from the floor to the ceiling on a tilted course. Next to it was a piece of wallpaper that veered in the opposite direction at an ever increasing angle. A bumpy, bubbly glob of paste bridged the gap between the two pieces. The walls looked like they had been covered by two year old children at a day care center. I panicked, unable to bring myself to tell him how bad it was, as well as wondering how he could not know that it was a disaster. The thought of his paying ten thousand dollars for this overwhelmed me. I told him that I would like to share my thoughts with Dr. Wayne. As Mohammed watched with concern, I reported to Wayne about the wallpaper. He just shrugged his shoulders.

"See, I told you it would be easy. Tell Mohammed what you just told me."

"Mohammed," I called, as I motioned him to approach.

"Yes?" he asked, as did three other men, who stepped forward.

"I think that you should fire the man whom you are using. Get someone else. No one else could be as bad as your current paperhanger. Even if he agreed to work for free, you should still fire him. My eight year old daughter could do a better job."

The exuberance he showed in expressing his appreciation for my expertise made me very uncomfortable. Wayne just kept laughing.

The next day in the clinic, my first patient was a teenage girl who was accompanied by her father. As she sat in the dental chair, I asked her to remove the veil covering her face. She did not understand what I asked, so turning to Mohammed, I asked him to translate. He explained that her father would not allow her to expose her face to me, as I was an infidel from the West.

"Mohammed, I can't examine and treat her unless I can see her mouth."

"You do not understand. Her father will not allow you to see her face."

We went back and forth. Finally, I suggested that Mohammed make a mask which covered everything the father wanted covered, but left an opening for the mouth.

"No, Dr. Toon, take the day off. I will treat this young lady, myself. Do not worry; I know what to do. I treat all of Dr. Nez's patients. He trained me."

I returned to the tented compound to find Rinnce jogging the perimeter. Her jogging outfit was offending many of the locals, so she terminated her run. We decided to take a bus to the beach. The men wore the briefest of brief styled bathing suits, while the women, wrapped like mummies, watched the men swim. As we sat on the beach, we heard the sounds and saw the lighted arcs of missiles flying between Hahakabia and Buhukastan, as the two countries resumed an unfinished war. We returned to the tented compound and decided to enter the nearby, gated town of Rahrahan. A large crowd was forming in the square to witness the stoning of a teenage girl, who had been raped by her uncle. We were told that the cultural presumption was that she was the one to be punished, as she must have tempted him.

We rushed back to the compound, where I went in search of Mohammed. When I finally found him, I told him that Rinnce and I had to get out of the country. It wasn't for us. He told us that he had to follow our prescribed schedule and that he was not authorized to help us make any changes. We returned to town and found a camel drawn carriage on ski like runners. The driver agreed to take us to the airport; however, he could only travel on sand through the dunes. It was getting dark and we feared that we might just end up entombed in one of Allah's sandcastles. Hahakabia Airlines charged us a severe penalty for the change in our return schedule. When we landed back in the States, we knew we had a story to tell that no one would believe. It didn't matter. We didn't believe it either. There was a message on our answering machine from Cougar Lugar, asking me to call her.

"I heard that you extracted yourselves early. What's wrong?," she asked, with a note of sadness.

"I met a guy named Rudyard Kipling, who kept whispering in my ear."

"That's a ridiculous reason to terminate the trip so early. If this guy Kipling was a lech, you should have just reported him to the authorities."

"He wasn't a lech, Cougar; He was a writer."

"It figures, all the writers I know are weird."

"He wasn't weird, Cougar; he was right. He told me that 'East is East, and West is West, and never the twain shall meet, till Earth and Sky stand presently at God's great Judgment Seat.'"

"What the hell are you talking about, Spit? You're sounding crazy. Did you get buried in a sand dune?"

"No, I just read the poem 'The Ballad of East and West,' by Rudyard Kipling."

"So, what does it mean?"

"It's too complicated to explain. Let's just say that I reacted to it literally, even though it's out of context."

"I'm not following you, Spit,"

"Yes, that's it, Cougar. You have gotten the real punch line of Kipling's words, which have challenged the greatest minds for over one hundred years."

"Well, if I have, I still don't know what it is."

"Sure you do, Cougar. You said it: 'I'm not following you.' That's the punch line. I'm not following you either. Moreover, I'm not following Gusher Oil, or Dr. Upton Nez, or patients with covered mouths, or camels, or sand castles, or stills that make 'Brown' and 'White'; or incompetent contractors who can't hang wallpaper; or the Hahakabian principles of justice which are written, not in stone, but with stonings."

"Well, other than those few minor glitches, which I'm sure we can address to your satisfaction, how was everything else?"

"Good luck, Cougar; take care. Don't bother to send me a check. I won't deposit it."

"May I check with you again, some other time, if another position in a different locale comes up?"

"No, Cougar, I'm all tapped out. The well is dry. Maybe, if I had a name like Cougar Lugar, I would consider wildcatting."

She didn't laugh, and she slammed the phone down hard.

ON THE ROAD AGAIN

Wanting to get the bad taste of gushing oil out of our mouths, Rinnce and I decided that there was only one sure mouthwash: France. We contacted Raoul and Monique in Paris, and Jean Marie and Mireille in Montpellier, to tell them to fill up their wine cellars and to book their favorite bistros and brasseries.

Rinnce, Spittella, and I boarded a plane for Nice. We arrived at the airport during some security crisis to be greeted by soldiers and machine guns. It wasn't the French *je ne sais quoi* that I had envisioned. The agent at the car rental counter advised me that the car I had reserved wasn't available, but that they had upgraded the reservation to a top of the line luxury *voiture*.

C'est merveilleux, I groaned, fearing that I wouldn't know how to start the vehicle. In fact, I didn't even know how to open the door. When I finally got myself into the driver's seat, it took a lot of trial and error screeching, grinding, and ripping sounds to get the car started and moving, although not very smoothly. The voiture jolted along, with us hanging on like cowboys on bucking broncos. I looked at the dials on the dashboard, clueless as to what they were trying to tell me.

"*Mon Dieu, merde*," I screamed. "We don't have any gas."

"Calm down, Spit, you always start with a full tank with a rental," Rinnce said, reassuringly," but I still didn't feel reassured.

"*Pas aujourd'hui*," I exclaimed, meaning "Don't bet your Armagnac on that today, baby. Our tank is empty, *vide*; it needs to be full, that is to say, *pleine*."

I stopped at a gas station, but I didn't understand most of the words on the pump. Trying to pump gas into the tank, I found that nothing, *rien*, happened. I turned to the Frenchman at the adjacent pump.

"*Pardon Monsieur, mais j'ai besoin d'assistance, s'il vous plait.*"

He frowned deeply. His message was clear: "Yankee go home." Reluctantly, he shuffled over and took the nozzle from my hand and squeezed the trigger. He looked at me like I was nuts.

"Monsieur, c'est pleine;" however, he said it in a way that meant: "You pathetic, American jerk; don't you know the damned tank is full. What the hell is wrong with you?"

"*Une mille mercis*," I said, kissing his hand and bowing with a flourish. Then, having offered him those thousand thank yous, I stood erect, saluted him, and sang the French National Anthem, *La Marseillaise*, which I followed with a click of my heels. He looked at me with his mouth agape. Tears ran down his cheeks. He stepped toward me, threw his arms around me, and kissed me one, two, and three times on the cheeks.

"*Vous êtes fou*," he said, which I understood to mean: "You are one crazy dingbat," which I took as a compliment.

"*Combien d'argent?*," I asked the cashier, as I walked into the station.

"*Je ne sais pas. C'etait seulement une goutte*," he answered. So, I gave him a franc for the one drop. He seemed happy enough with that.

We were finally on the road. It was too early to check into the hotel, so we drove to Cannes; or maybe it was St. Tropez. They look alike to me. We rented some chaise lounges for the beach, and we changed our clothes in a cabana. Rinnce and Spittella stretched out to capture their tans. I began jogging along the water's edge. The beach was covered with bare breasts, more bare breasts than any American male deserved or could comprehend. As I ran straight along the water, my head was turned ninety degrees to the left to keep abreast of the breasts. I didn't hear the calls at first, but they increased in volume and number.

"*Attention Monsieur*! *Attention Monsieur*!"

They were telling me to be careful, to watch out for something, and that I was in danger. I looked around, but too late. The pier about which they were trying to warn me was in the process of following the rules of physics. I crashed into it, and with an equal and opposite reaction, I bounced backwards onto the warm, welcoming sand, where I lay out cold. When I regained consciousness, I was looking straight into the eyes of a young woman about 20. As she was topless, I didn't notice the color of her eyes.

"*Bonjour Monsieur*; *bienvenue à France*," she said beautifully.

It was a welcome that would stay with me for days. My headache spoke the words of welcome to me over and over again: "bienvenue, bienvenue, bienvenue." It was like a French drummer banging in syncopation, a rhythm that puts an emphasis on a beat, or a subdivision of a beat, that is not usually emphasized. It was apparent that my headache was that beat. Rinnce and Spittella didn't miss a beat in trying to see who could show the least amount of sympathy for my pain.

The next day, we were driving along *les corniches*, the winding roads carved into the mountains where on one side is the mountain wall, and on the other is the sea. I noted that only I seemed to know about the existence of automotive brakes. Nary a car, except mine, showed any glimmer in its brake lights. Unlike my beach run, I kept my eyes glued straight, because every time I looked out over the ledge to the sea, the car would follow my eyes. The screams from Rinnce and Spittella were not good for my headache, but they did save our lives.

We traveled toward Montpellier, but as we approached Aix-en-Provence, we decided to stop for lunch. Parking the car on a pretty, shady street, we walked into town, enjoyed the sights, and sat under an umbrella, al fresco, while dining on fruits of the sea. We started to walk back to our car, but we had no idea where we were, how to get back to the car, or the name of the street where we had parked. Wandering about aimlessly, I finally bit the bullet, swallowed my male pride, and approached a gendarme about our dilemma. He gave me the same look of disdain as the fellow at the gas pump.

"It's a pretty, shady street with green trees and red brick apartment buildings."

"*Oui, Monsieur, comme tout le ville*," he said, not trying to hide his exasperation.

"Oui, like all the streets in the whole city," I said, agreeably.

The three of us got into his police car, and he began driving around the city. Eventually, we found our car. It had been right around the corner from where we had started our long search with him. I tried my routine of appreciation which had worked so well at the gas pump. This time, I didn't get an embrace or see him shed a tear. He didn't say that I was crazy. I wasn't quite sure what the French word he kept saying to me meant, but I think he was calling me an asshole.

We made it to Montpellier, and we connected with Jean Marie and Mireille, who had a house in Palavas-les-Flots, as well as an apartment at La Grande-Motte. They put us up in their apartment. The next day Rinnce, Spittella, and I; along with Jean Marie and Mireille's daughter Sylvie, drove through Languedoc.

Now, my modus operandi for historic locales and art museums is to keep on moving through them. Remember, I'm a big picture guy. The detail of information that everyone seems to have an obsession to share is way beyond my needs.

The morning went well until we stopped at Chateau Beaubelle. A uniformed docent would not let us just take a peek. He insisted on escorting us around. While the docent spoke French that even Sylvie did not understand, we marched through every room, closet, attic, basement, garden, stable, and *pissoir*. Each time I tried to say *merci* and *au revoir*, the docent would grab my hand and say "*Non monsieur, pas encore. Ce n'est pas le fin.*" Well, as far as I was concerned, it was the end before it began, but we were stuck. We finally got back on the road, our schedule in shambles. Decades later, I can still picture the officious little bugger leading us around as he babbled away to unreceptive ears and minds.

The day came when we had to say good-bye to our hosts. We were scheduled to return our rental car to the agency, which was conveniently located at the train station from where we were going to take the TGV bullet train to Paris. We headed to the station, only to discover major road work in progress along the way, with numerous detours to follow. We got stuck in traffic jams, ended up on one way streets going the wrong way, and began to suffer the effects of rising blood pressure. When we got to the train station, we learned that the rental agency had moved to a new location, for which someone scrawled the address on the back of a matchbook while mumbling the directions. We drove up and down the streets of Montpellier in search of the new location. At last, Rinnce saw the sign for the agency, but nowhere to park. While Rinnce double parked, I ran into the office to find out what to do.

"Just leave the auto *sur le trottoir*," the man behind the counter said.

"On the sidewalk?," I repeated.

"Oui," he said.

"*Ou*," I said, which meant "where the devil am I going to put it?"

"*La bas*," he pointed, using his middle finger, which to this day I think was purposeful, although all our French friends tell me that his finger meant nothing, because they use the pounded bent arm, *le bras d'honneur*, to express disrespect while saying 'va te faire foutre.' Well, I certainly wasn't going to va te faire foutre myself, that's for sure! Thanks to Raoul's échange culturel, I understood the meaning of that phrase as easily as eating *gâteau chocolat*. Anyway, I drove up onto the sidewalk to where he had pointed.

Not having much time left to catch our train, I asked the rental agent if he could help us get to the station quickly.

"But Monsieur, the station is right across the street," he said, pointing with that damned middle finger again. We made the train just as it was getting ready to pull out.

We spent seven glorious days in Paris. I stuck to my guns. We saw the Louvre in twenty minutes. Versailles took a little longer, but not much. We did linger; however, in the bistros and brasseries, drinking Sancerre and Beaujolais, while eating bouillabaisse, pot au feu, and cassoulet. We walked through the parks and the gardens. We sailed on the Seine. It was *la vie en rose*: life as seen through rose colored glasses and lived at Spit Toon's Saloon.

The trip to France was not our first, nor would it be our last, but it was the last time that we rented a car. The adventures of traveling, which I found so easy in my younger days, became more burdensome with age. With fear and trepidation, Rinnce and I took our first, of what would be many, escorted bus and boat tours of Europe. After the first tour, we knew that it was the only way we would be traveling in the future. There was no stress, no worries, no baggage issues, no language obstacles, and no getting lost. However, there was way too much information, which was detailed, repeated, compared, contrasted, analyzed, notarized, and plagiarized. I must confess, though, that it really was nice to learn so much about so many people, places, and things, that I had either zipped by or been ignorantly unaware.

One day, while in London walking through Harrod's, I stopped to ask a young salesman, who was dressed in tails, if he could direct me to the bathrooms.

"Would that be to buy or to use?," he inquired, as Rinnce began to laugh in her very special way.

On a trip through Spain, while our fellow travelers sucked up the history of crumbling walls, we would suck up wine in tapas bars or wander through art galleries.

We were in no hurry to return to the trials and tribulations of the daily grind.

TRIALS AND TRIBULATIONS

I'd always thought of jury duty as being like continuing dental education, a necessary and noble obligation, but always so inconvenient. So, when I got the call to appear for night court, I dutifully, but not happily, went forth to insure that truth and justice would be served.

I sat in a large waiting area, one of about sixty potential jurors. The jury was to be only six members. I was relieved to see that I would not be one of them, but then the assistant district attorney, after a rather pointed exchange with one of the selected jurors, opted for her dismissal. Another juror had to be chosen. The judge stood behind the bench and drew a name from a box.

"Salvatore Spittell Toon," he called.

I shook my head in dismay, thinking how I really didn't need this now.

"For the information of all present," the judge continued, "I have personally known Dr. Toon for many years, and I consider him to be a friend. I do not feel that this should, in any way, interfere with either of us carrying out our duties fairly and responsibly."

I was instructed to sit with the jurors. The assistant district attorney stood up from behind his table and walked toward the jury box.

"Dr. Toon, do you feel that you can fairly and objectively sit in judgment of an ex-convict?"

"Yes," I responded, as the juror beside me whispered "Dope! You should have said no."

"Is there anything that you would like to tell the court which you feel we should know about you?," the assistant district attorney asked.

"Yes, in addition to being a friend of the judge, I know the defendant."

"In what capacity?"

"I buy my gas at his gas station."

"Oh my God, why can't I be as lucky as you?," was the whisper I had expected and which was delivered.

"Anything else?"

"Yes."

"Go ahead."

"I know the defense attorney."

"Send us a postcard," wafted overhead in a familiar whisper.

"In what context do you know the defense attorney?"

"Socially. I've been at several events with him."

"Like what?"

"Dinner parties, weddings, and stuff like that."

"If I may address the court," the defense attorney said, as he rose from his chair. "It is true that Dr. Toon and I are socially acquainted, but not to any degree that will preclude his ability to serve on the jury."

"Welcome back," came the expected whisper.

The judge, the assistant district attorney, and the defense attorney all left the room to huddle. Within seconds they were back, and the words to swear me in as a juror rang loud and clear through the courtroom.

The plaintiff, until this moment unknown and unseen, appeared. He was an intimidating figure who was on parole. When the plaintiff had tried to rob money, at gunpoint, from the defendant's gas station, the defendant had beaten him to a pulp with a baseball bat which he kept under the cash register. The plaintiff filed aggravated assault charges against the defendant.

The jurors, who were not supposed to communicate among themselves, looked at each other in utter dismay, all thinking the same words at the same time: "What is this all about?"

The trial took two nights. During the proceedings, a very rough looking group of supporters for the plaintiff made their presence clearly known. Late on the second night, the judge spent an hour droning on about the jury's duties for deliberation. Behind closed doors, we sat down at a table. No one spoke or moved.

"Let's each indicate, on a piece of paper, whether we think the defendant is guilty or innocent of each of the three counts against him," I suggested.

The six of us made a total of 18 notations of innocent.

"Well, I guess that's it," I said. "Let's deliver the news and get out of here."

"But we haven't even deliberated, and I'm the foreman. We can't go out there after only about thirty seconds behind closed doors. It won't look good," one of the jurors whined.

"Someone send out for pizza and beer," four other jurors groaned.

We found a deck of cards and played a few hands of poker, while chatting among ourselves as if we were at a cocktail party.

"That's enough time; let's go," I said, looking at my watch.

"I'm supposed to say that, the foreman complained," in an irritating, nasal sounding voice.

"So said and so heard," the rest of us snapped in unison.

"Have you reached a verdict?," the judge asked, in a voice of authority.

"Well, yes, more or less, although we didn't deliberate in the classic fashion. I guess we still got it right, in a reverse sort of way, though," our foreman sniveled.

"Mistrial, mistrial," the assistant district attorney cried, as he jumped to his feet sounding like Emile Zola, shouting "*J'accuse, J'accuse!*," many years ago in defense of Alfred Dreyfus.

The judge met with the jury in his chambers. When he returned, he declared a mistrial. A new trial was scheduled for the succeeding week with a different jury.

"How do you find?" the judge asked them after they deliberated.

"We find the defendant guilty on two counts: using a corked bat and not swinging harder. Most importantly, we find the judge and the district attorney guilty of wasting the people's time and money, for which you both must pay by taking the fall for disrespecting us all. That is our verdict and final call."

RUNNING ON EMPTY

I had already entered two marathons, but I had failed to finish either one. Everyone was telling me that not only must I enter a third marathon, but that, "no matter how ugly," I must finish it to get "the monkey off my back." So, I started training with a group of guys at the local running club, but I couldn't keep up with any of them.

"Spit, you need more than physical training. You need to see a sports psychologist. It's your last hope to stick it to the monkey," several of the members advised. On their advice, I went to see Minimus Shrinnkk.

"Imagery will maximize your chances," Minimus said. "You've got to imagine yourself as Phidippides, that Greek runner who ran all over Greece looking for help from the Spartans to do battle with the Persians on the plains of Marathon. That should enhance your visceral sensation of being fully in the moment and give you that extra boost for which you are looking."

"If I'm not mistaken, that guy died after running 26 miles to Athens," I felt obligated to note.

"Well, yes, technically, but we're talking imagery."

"So imagery can trump technically?"

"I imagine so," Minimus replied.

On the day of the race, I waited at the back of the pack, 25,000 strong, for the starting gun to fire. Fifteen minutes passed before I had space to take my first step. Thirty minutes ticked off on my watch before I crossed the starting line. I didn't imagine that I was Phidippides, but I imagined that the runner in front of me was. I decided that all I had to do was run side by side and stride for stride with him. But every time I pulled up beside the runner in front of me, there was another runner still ahead. So I would speed up to overtake the next Phidippides. Before I could say Souvlaki, I was out of gas. My mind said "run," but my legs didn't listen. My voice screamed "move," but my feet sank deeper into the pavement. I lifted and pushed each leg, one at a time. I felt a monkey place his hands on my shoulders.

While the aged, the infirm, and the physically challenged all waved to me in passing, the only imagery I could conjure up was jogging around the air base compound in Vietnam every evening with a group of physicians and dentists. I heard my roommate Tenn Dunn, an orthopedic surgeon, noting that, as we were all Eagle Scouts, we were victims of a military conspiracy to conscript the brightest and the best. I remembered how I made it known that I had not gotten my War Merit Badge and that this fact, when brought to light, would provide the grounds for me to go home. As it turned out, my grounds were beyond baseless; they were quicksand.

Darkness fell as I finally fell across the finish line. I was too wasted to relish the moment, but I did realize that it was a good news, bad news moment. The good news was that I had finally completed a marathon. The bad news was that I had finished ugly — very ugly. The good news was that the monkey was off my back. The bad news was that even though I used every last ounce of energy to stomp on the monkey, he looked at me with disgust. His eyes rolled and he stuck out his tongue. Then, with a shriek that only a monkey could make, he gave me the finger, not only with disdain, but with extreme prejudice as well. I tried to imagine that I was dead, but it didn't work. Then I imagined that Minimus was dead. That worked a little better.

Gristmill Wall

Chipped mortar lines scarred
a lone stone wall: a remnant
of a gristmill ground away
by the winds of time.
Split wooden rails reached
out from the wall and slalomed
between the fence's posts.
I stretched out my arms and ran
like the flight of a bird, my feet
lifting off the narrow, runway
strip between the fence and the
creek.
My fingers strummed the harp-like
strings of the splintering rails in
the rhythm of the baton branching
out from an orchestral tree.
On a chair of rock, with the
the sounds of water rushing
over my feet, I whittled on
a piece of driftwood.
I wondered if I could stand as tall,
and with as much dignity, as the
gristmill wall while the winds of
time whittled on me.

HUDDLE

He wasn't the man he used to be;
the glory of his past had waned.
No longer could he run as far, as
fast, or as frequently, as in his days
of fame.
But despite the toll of the passing
years, he still followed his historic
patterns by walking the gridiron
sidewalks of the city in which he
lived.
Walking down and out along an
avenue, he would suddenly cut
right or left onto a street as called
in the huddle of his mind. And
farther along, he relished the
reverse he would make and then
his hand-off to another, from whom
a flea-flicker would be launched in
surprise.
But his greatest joy was looking at the
sky where an oval sun spiraled over his
shoulder and dropped gently into his
outstretched hands as he crossed the line
to his goal: the front door of his apartment,
where he kicked off his shoes, poured his
aperitif, and enjoyed the satisfying
point-after.

BRIAN-BRIAN

I watched our 14 year old daughter Spittella play in a round-robin drill at the tennis club. It was very obvious that her hormones zoned in on one specific guy across the net from her. Each time they were paired, the level of her game rose to near professional levels. The hormonal levels of her male opponent responded to the challenge by opening his eyes wide with wonder and dropping his jaw to the floor with lustful infatuation. Storm clouds passed through my mind, and on the way home I asked her about "Jaw Dropper."

"Who?," she asked, in the most blasé manner she could muster.

"You know, the heavy hitter drooling out of both sides of his mouth who kept stepping on his tongue."

"Sorry, Dad, I'm drawing a blank."

"Picture 'Mouth Drooler,' aka 'Tongue Stepper,' although you may only remember him as the lech at whom you hit your professional level forehand right between his eyes."

"Oh yeah, what about him?"

"What's his name?"

"Brrriiiaaannn," she oozed, squeezing out every grain of sugar from its oh so sweet sound.

The storm clouds that had passed through my mind did a u-turn, returned, and then thickened. And so began Spittella's seven and a half year romance — a nail biting match of double faults, foot faults, and missed line calls, during which Rinnce and I held our breath while hanging precariously from a precipice. We wanted to tear out our hair; but we couldn't, because our fingernails were preoccupied with holding onto the cliff's edge. However, our hair had a mind of its own, and needing no help from anyone or anything else, it whitened nicely in a very short period of time.

Although it was a close line call, Spittella and Brrriiiaaannn finally acknowledged that tennis and hormones were really all that they had in common, and they went their separate ways. Ironically though, Spittella ended up marrying a guy whose name was also Brrriiiaaannn.

To keep the Brrriiiaaannns straight, I renamed them Brian One and Brian Two, but instead of calling my son-in-law Brian Two, I called him Brian-Brian.

"You need to stop calling Brian, Brian-Brian. I want you to just call him Brian," Spittella implored.

"But that's Brian One's name, isn't it?," I questioned.

"You can call Brian One, Brian-Brian, if it makes you happy, but I want you to stop calling Brian Two, Brian-Brian. Just call him Brian, okay?"

"How can I do that? Your husband appeared on the scene after Brian One, so that makes him Brian Two, or Brian-Brian."

"Look at it this way, Dad. You never see Brian One anymore, and you most likely never will. You see Brian Two constantly. He's the number one Brian in my life. Brian One came in second, for which you should be very happy. So just rename Brian One as Brian-Brian, and just rename Brian Two as Brian.

"Point, game, set, match, Ms. Toon," I announced. "Give my regards to Bri," I added.

THE MEASURE OF A MAN

She took the measure of a man
by what measures he took to
measure up.
Was he a man upon whom she
could count, or was he simply
the calculating type?
Moreover, was he someone
whose sum total of traits added
up to his being an exponential
power in her life, while she
remained number one in his?
She believed that she had
gauged him accurately,
although deep down inside
she worried that her algorithm
might have skewed the statistics.
She decided to think it out again,
being extra careful not to go off
on a new tangent.

TAPS

The sky was dark, the air was cold, and hearts were heavy on this Valentine's Day. The bugle's sad notes hung over the grave as family and friends bid farewell to my father-in-law, Bourne Wehl. A singer's voice faded out and faded in: "Day is done, gone the sun... All is well, safely rest, God is nigh."

The five uniformed military veterans who were present to fulfill Bourne's wishes for a military funeral joined family and friends at Bourne's country club for a luncheon reception. As I was just sinking my teeth into a deliciously rare piece of roast beef, my brother-in-law tapped me on the shoulder.

"I told the vets about your Vietnam service," he said. "They want to meet you.

"Jeez, oh man," I groaned. "They're going to have a bird when they hear my stories."

"Oh, just humor them," my brother-in-law snapped, a little too strongly.

"Easy for you to say, draft-dodger, I spit back."

"Evader," my brother-in-law corrected.

"Well, at least I served, so I guess it's better me than you," I sighed.

"Make us proud, Captain," my brother-in-law said, saluting.

I greeted the vets with a hearty hello, firm handshakes, and much appreciation for their service to the country. They wanted to know all about my tour of duty.

"Listen guys," I said, defensively, "I've got to be perfectly honest with you. I served unhappily, I did my time, and I did it well; but I wasn't a gung-ho military man like you guys were and are. Picture Hawkeye Pierce and B.J. Hunnicutt in the movie and television series *MASH*. That was pretty much what my life was like over there."

"What do you mean," one of them asked.

"I mean that I was in the Dental Corps. We weren't considered real soldiers. We didn't buy into the military persona. We did what we had to do as health professionals, not as toy soldiers. We didn't salute; we didn't wear our hats; we argued with our commanders; we ruffled feathers; and we scrambled egg insignias on Colonels' hats.

We walked about anywhere, without permission, acting as if we were still in private practice back in the U.S.A."

I listened politely to their stories, which were so much more heroic than mine. After each one, I would counter with an irreverent story which mocked what they espoused. They too were very polite, nodding and smiling, but obviously a little blind-sided by my perspective. Finally, I excused myself and returned to my table. A half hour later, my brother-in-law tapped me on the shoulder, again.

"They want to talk with you some more."

"No they don't," I said. "They're horrified by my not taking the military seriously enough."

"No, they liked your stories. They want to hear more."

"This is getting tiresome, but they deserve respect and appreciation, unlike you," I said.

"Very funny, Salvatore," my brother-in-law replied, with an edge of hostility. He always called me Salvatore when I was getting under his skin.

I returned for my encore, where I was greeted with enthusiasm.

"Tell us some more stuff that we don't want to hear. It's very funny, even if it appalls us," one of the vets said.

And, so began another hour of one tale after another: accidentally dropping an M-16 from a helicopter into enemy rice paddies below, as I flew with my roommate, the orthopedic surgeon Tenn Dunn; refusing to see a General at midnight for a root canal, and then telling him to take an aspirin and to see me in the morning; dining out with different military units because their food was better than the Air Force cuisine; and going into DaNang, which was off-limits, for dinner and nightclubs. They couldn't hear enough, but I had had enough. We embraced, and I promised to look them up the next time I was in town, which I didn't. I felt more sad, rather than bad, about not seeing these men, because they were the real soldiers whose lives were used foolishly by our government. They were real decent men who were locked into memories of a difficult life: a life from which they could not let go. They deserved better. I knew that I was lucky. If I had to go to Vietnam, at least I went as a dentist, and as a Captain in the Air Force, assigned to a large air base that just so happened to have a club named DOOM. I didn't suffer like these men and so many others like them whom I met over the course of my life.

As I lay in bed that night, reflecting on the events of the day, I marveled at how my Vietnam experience created an instant bond with other combat zone veterans, regardless of who they were and what they did. Sharing the experience of being in a war, in a far distant land, defined a part of one's life in a way that only those who had done the same could understand.

EPITAPH

A cold wind blew through the cemetery's
canals of tall grass, causing each blade
to bend in mourning.
Stalactite tears hung from tombstone
eyes, as memories darted about
like kites in the sky.
The epitaph spoke with the sound of
his voice: "Good life, good death,
good-bye."

BUBBLES

To say that Rinnce and I were excited would be a skosh short of the mark. Actually, we were revved and ready to roll. We drove out of the dental office parking lot strewing 35 years of responsibilities out of the car window as if they were ticker tape. As we headed into the sunset, we were blinded more by our dreams than by the sun itself.

Bubbling over with happiness, we opened a bottle of first class bubbly, a real deal Champagne straight from Epernay. I picked up the phone and called our realtor. "Let's do it," I said. "Put the house for sale sign up tomorrow and let the bidding begin."

The morning headline was "Real estate bubble bursts." Rinnce and I heard the whoosh of water gushing from our waterbed. The realtor said to sell low and to get out fast. There were no offers made, and we were stuck. We took the house off the market and decided to stay put.

The very next day a man knocked on the door and said he wanted to buy the house. He offered a fair price, which we accepted. Although we should have been bubbly with relief, it was frustration that bubbled through our veins, as the buyer was a bit of a bubblehead with whom to deal.

When Rinnce and I walked out of the house for the very last time, we were bubbling over with excitement and tickled with delight. Bubbles have a way of doing that.

A GLASS OF GRAMERCY

Our new townhouse stood on a well groomed, tree lined street. Our neighbors on each side of us were retirees who, like us, had relocated to be near their children and grandchildren. With confluent timing and so much in common, we were destined to become close friends.

Rinnce and I had left our vineyard behind, over which we had toiled futilely for ten years, turning out inferior wine which many thought could be used as a military defoliant. I had compensated for this through marketing. I replaced my corks with baby style nipple tops and renamed the wine "Suck and Savor."

Rinnce had always dreamed of retiring to a high-rise in Gramercy Park in New York City, but my marketing concept had failed. Financial reality brought us to a suburban street which ironically was named Gramercy Lane. Our townhouse backed onto a steep, unmaintained hill, the crest of which was bordered by a split rail fence. I planted a grapevine adjacent to each vertical post of the fence, ultimately trellising the horizontal growth along its length.

The bonsai vineyard, looking no more grand than a lonely flower in a single pot, became the symbolic connection of Gramercy Lane, where any glass of wine was referred to as "a glass of Gramercy."

We were thrilled with the high style and active depth of our new life. But while it brought us much joy, it also gave us a feeling of guilt. I, who was used to mowing my own lawn, was surprised to see a landscaping contractor arrive daily with Los Mexicanos to take care of all things outdoor around the complex. I felt sorry for the workers, so much more disadvantaged than us, and I was worried that they were being exploited. I sought advice from a therapist, Dr. Noel Moore Gilt, a non-participating provider in our health plan, who advised me to hum the uplifting score from the musical *Les Miserables.* Instead, I learned how to roll my *r*'s in words like Torremolinos. I began standing on the front porch handing out placards, giving fiery speeches in broken Spanish, and organizing the workers for whom I began to negotiate with bosses who were none too pleased.

Rinnce studied Spanish guitar, learned to make tapas, to dance Flamenco, and to make sure that "a glass of Gramercy" was frequently a Rioja, a Rueda, or a Ribera del Duero wine.

Our new neighbors across the street were French and heavily into Armagnac. Although the women found it too strong for their taste, all the men loved it. History repeated itself as the Armagnac bottles would be drained in one evening, rather than in the traditional extended periods to which our French neighbors were accustomed. We wasted no time in trying to make them understand that Armagnac was more than an after dinner drink.

"It is also a delightful choice of bottle from which to fill 'a glass of Gramercy,'" we would say in response to our hosts' complaints.

COWBOYS, INDIANS, AND BROTHELS

It was her eyes, those dark, flirtatious, come-hither eyes, that grabbed you by the throat and in the heart while silently saying "Hey, cowboy, you're my kind of guy; whatta ya say?" I said "Hop in beautiful; let's take a ride." She sat quietly, taking me in with one eye, while looking out the window with the other.

Despite the rather garish bow in her hair, and a perfume that was way too strong for my nose and reeking havoc with my genetic code for allergic reaction, there was no doubt that she was a very special damsel who evoked nobility like no other. I lowered the window on my side of the car to flush out the allergens, but as I continued to sneeze, I was forced to lower the window on her side of the car as well. As the wind blew through her hair, she looked even more beautiful than before, especially when she would look over at me with those seductive eyes.

I dropped her off at her house, and then I made my way home.

"Oh my, where have you been, or more precisely, with whom have you been? You smell like a French brothel," my wife of 42 years observed, playfully.

"Mon Dieu, ma chérie, but how would you, of all people, know what a French brothel smells like?," I returned, glad that her first serve was in.

"A woman knows," she volleyed back. "I must confess that I am quite disappointed that my Eagle Scout husband would enter such a place. Do you have an itch?," she asked quizzically.

"An itch?," I repeated. "What on earth are you talking about?"

"You know, the guy thing: the seven year itch, wandering eyes, and old man dreams."

"I may be an old man, but I am still a man, and real men with proper testosterone levels appreciate beauty. Our eyes do not wander; they scan in wonder and appreciation," I replied, enjoying the sustained rally.

"Oh, pulleeeze! I bet that you'll give me an equally colorful explanation for the hairs all over your clothes," my wife smashed back at me right on the baseline.

"Well, yes, I can explain that," I replied out of breath as my run to her return fell short of the ball.

"I'm sure you can," my wife said, with more derision than I would have expected from the mother of our only child. So, tell me about LaLa, or Lulu, or Lola, or whatever her name is."

"The lady's name is Sheesho," I stated curtly.

"Sheesho, what kind of name is that?"

"Shichon," I replied smugly.

"She's a Native American, a Shoshone Indian?" my wife asked incredulously.

"No, she's a Shichon, not a Shoshone," I corrected..

"Shichon, Shoshone, whatever."

"Well," I cut in. "I don't think a Shoshone Indian would take kindly to being called a Shichon."

"Why not?"

"Because a Shichon is a dog."

"I've never heard of a Shichon dog,"

"It's a cross between a Shih Tzu and a Bichon Frise."

"I've never heard of either one of them," she admitted. "So, you're trying to make me believe that your friend from the French brothel is a dog?"

"*Au contraire*, she is lovely, as well as being a dog."

"I give up," my wife exclaimed. "I'm listening. Tell me the story."

"You give up way too fast these days, *ma chérie*. *Peut-être* it is you who are aging, *pas moi*. It is really a very simple tale. Our French neighbors were in a bind and asked if I would pick up their dog, Sheesho, at the groomer and drop her off at their house on my way home. The poor creature was distraught at having been left in that horrid emporium where they sheered her naked, wrapped her in god awful ribbon, and sprayed her with what one could call 'Eau de French Brothel.' Sheesho couldn't stand all the loose hairs all over her naked body and kept shaking herself in my car, setting off an explosion of white hairs that not only settled all over the upholstery, but on my clothes as well."

"Point, game, set, match: Mr. Wonderful," my wife announced with a smile. "Great match, darling — just like us.

Her dark eyes glistened flirtatiously with that come-hither look. She helped me off with my aromatic, dog hair covered clothes; threw them in the hamper, took my hand, and led me to the boudoir.

"Woof, woof."

WOOF, WOOF, WOOF

A pain shot through my jaw
awakening me from my sleep,
while my wife lay beside me
in a slumber sound and deep.
Out of bed I slipped real quick
in search of a pill I could pick
to stop the pain which I felt
and end my spiral, downward melt.
One didn't work, so I took another,
and then I prayed to the Holy Mother,
but instead of the pain going away,
it came back stronger with more to say.
Still in my pajamas, I ran outside
from the blinding pain to try to hide,
but stride for stride it kept up with me,
until there was nothing I could see.
Unable to view where I went,
on some step the night I spent
from where I howled at the moon
hoping help would find me soon.
I passed out oblivious to all
until I heard a siren's call
and saw red lights atop a car
flashing at me from afar.
A man in white jumped out at me
looking like a dentist to set me free.
"No, I'm a vet," he said with a scowl.
"You sounded like a dog with that howl."
He tapped my bicuspid and I jumped real high,
but he caught my leg before I reached the sky.
He pulled me down and pulled my tooth way up,
and then I heard it fall into a metal cup.
I licked his hand and wagged my tail
and let out a joyous, reverberating wail
that soared to a nearby shingled roof,
only to be followed by a woof, woof, woof.

"NUCLEAR" AND "ENERGY"

I'm no nuclear scientist, so I haven't had any experience with nuclear energy; however, I do have lots of experience with "Nuclear" and "Energy." That's what I call my two grandsons: Ian and Oren. They call me "Pa," except when I'm with "Ma," and then we become the singular two-headed "PaMa."

Granted, the world has changed since I was their age, but even at the top of my form, I never equaled their per second energy output. When I am with them, I feel like I am in a rowboat with oars chasing a rocket, as I try to catch what was fueled by fusion or fission with my "fishin pole."

I gave Ma a high five as I entered, and as she exited, our daughter Spittella's house. I couldn't help but notice that Ma's perfectly coiffed hair was a bit less perfect, her sparkling clean clothes were a bit less clean, and her usually vibrant expression was a bit more strained. She and I divided this regular two hour babysitting session into two one hour segments, believing that we were conserving our collective energy, even though we were starting to believe that we were just splitting the atom and creating a bigger boom.

Energy, the three year old, tackled me as soon as I entered the room. He hung onto my leg, creating a body surfing effect as his belly slid across the ceramic tiled floor as I huffed and puffed while dragging him, a weight which seemed to me like the stone of Sisyphus. At the same time, six year old Nuclear grabbed my arm and begged that I pitch batting practice to him in the backyard. Piper, the family dog, scampered among the three of us, causing me to stumble and fall, placing me under my two grandsons and the dog. I heard my cell phone ringing, but I couldn't pull it from my pocket, as Nuclear lay across one arm and Energy lay across the other. It kept ringing until I got my arm free.

"Dad, what's happening, why didn't you answer the phone? Is there a problem?"

"Everything is normal," I gasped, as I lay on my back on the floor in a wrestling pin, with a knee pressing against my Adam's apple.

"What did you say?"

"Everything is normal," I repeated in a faint rasp, as I became lightheaded.

"Dad, I can't hear or understand you. Are you having a heart attack or a stroke?"

"I should be so lucky," I gasped softly.

The sound of Mom's wheels screeching into the driveway caught everyone's ear. As she bounded through the front door and into the family room, the two boys were sitting peacefully on the sofa, with Piper between them, watching the Wiggles on television.

"How did it go?," Ma asked when I staggered through the door.

"No surprises. Everything was as usual," I said, as my hands were shaking as I poured myself some Armagnac. "But, you know Ma, I'm thinking of writing to President Obama and telling him about a great source of alternative energy."

MACARONI AND CHEESE

Four year old Energy was getting antsy. He was hungry, his mother wasn't home, and Rinnce and I were babysitting together. We told him he had to wait for lunch because we all were going to a restaurant as soon as his mother returned.

"I want my lunch now," Energy proclaimed in his infamous toddler tone of disagreement.

"I think I hear your Mom's car as we speak," I said, with my hand cupped over my ear.

"I don't hear her car," Energy whined.

"You're not listening carefully enough," I said. Cup your hand over your ear like this, stand on the front porch, and concentrate."

"I still can't hear her car," Energy announced, pouting.

"Yes, she's coming. I hear her car, but it's still kind of faraway. It sounds like she's near the supermarket. So, she won't be long now. Can you hear her, Energy?"

"I think so. Which restaurant are we going to?"

"Well, why don't we make a list of all your favorite ones, and then pick your most favorite?"

"Rocco's is my 'favoritist'; we don't need to make a list."

"Rocco's it is. And guess who's home?"

"I want macaroni and cheese — and uh — French fries, lemonade, and chocolate ice cream," Energy stated with utmost certainty to the waitress at Rocco's.

"His diet is so bad!," Ma groaned.

"Oren, you can't have lemonade and ice cream: just one or the other. Which do you want?," our daughter Spittella piped in, with appropriate authority.

"Uh, I want ice cream!"

"Okay, then you'll have water instead of lemonade. But you can't have French fries. They don't go with mac and cheese," his mother stated with the sagacity of a graduate from the Culinary Institute of America.

"They go," Energy whined, as he gave his pre-meltdown look, but the feared tantrum misfired and all seemed well. Becoming more agitated as the seconds ticked away, he cried "Where's my macaroni and cheese?"

"The chef has to make each noodle, one at a time, and he has to cook them in hot water, and he has to rub the melted cheese on each noodle, and that takes time," I explained.

"I want it now," Energy screamed, banging his spoon on the table.

"Listen," I said, "the noodles are hollering in the kitchen and hopping up and down in the hot water trying to get out of the pot, but the chef keeps pushing them back in."

Energy looked at me with just the hint of a smile, and then he instantly snarled that it was time for them to get out of the pot and come to him. He put his head on the table and began to whimper.

"Hooray!," Ma and Mom cheered. "The noodles are coming!"

Energy threw his arms up with glee. A second later he shrieked "They're too hot!"

The steam subsided as his mother, his grandmother, and his grandfather stirred, fanned, and blew. Energy's spoon finally rose to his mouth. His smile radiated everywhere: the same place his noodles were going.

CRAPS

When my grandson Energy was three, he saw a man at the supermarket put money into a scratch-off lottery ticket vending machine. As he wriggled free from my left hand, the box of eggs fell out of the bag in my right hand. He raced to the machine and pushed several buttons. A ticket popped out. Energy ran off with the ticket, with the man and me in hot pursuit. The man stepped on the box of eggs I had dropped. The gooey egg whites and yolks greased the floor, launched him upward, and caught him as he fell flat on his back. As people ran to his aid, I continued the chase. With the aid of several shoppers who surrounded Energy with their shopping carts, I was finally able to grab him.

"You have to give the nice man his ticket," I explained in a surprisingly calm tone, as Energy made his displeasure known with a world class tantrum. However, it was too late, as an ambulance was already racing the man to the hospital.

The ticket that Energy had snatched turned out to be a $30,000 winner. The local paper ran a front page piece about the incident with a photo of Energy holding the winning check. When the man read the article, he threw a world class tantrum, contacted the Lottery Office, and claimed that the money was his.

My daughter told the Lottery Office that she agreed with the man, whose name was Craps Hazard. However, the Lottery Office believed that Craps was only entitled to half of the money, as there was no way to know if he would have selected the same button that Energy pressed.

Craps was not happy with the compromise. As a scratch-off lottery ticket addict, he could not walk by a vending machine that sold scratch-off lottery tickets without buying one. He rarely got a winner. When he did, it was either for a free ticket or just a few dollars at most. He had lost a lot of money, owed a lot of money, and was in a lot of trouble with his creditors and his wife. His clothes were constantly covered with the scrapings from his tickets. He suffered from carpal tunnel syndrome, a repetitive stress injury to the wrist from all the tickets he scratched using a coin, as well as from all the dice he tossed at the craps table. With a life so invested, with so little reward, he now felt cheated.

My daughter, in fact, sent him her half of the winnings. "It was what the daughter of an Eagle Scout should do," I told her. Moreover, she included an extra fifty cents as it was Crap's dollar that paid for the ticket.

Poor Craps did not win an injury suit against the supermarket, and he never got a winning ticket again.

THE HORSE ZOO

"We're babysitting the two boys all day on Saturday," Rinnce called out, as she hung up the phone.

"All day? We'd better find something good and time consuming to entertain them," I noted, sweating ever so slightly.

I checked in with my activities adviser, "Coach Google," to see what was out there that would keep their blinking eyes staring, their fidgety bodies still, and their toothless smiles wide.

"Hey, the Pesky Proscenium Players are doing *Peter Pan* on Saturday," I announced with relief.

"That's awfully far to drive," Rinnce pointed out.

"Well, that's good. It burns up more time," I explained. "Add that to the right lunch, in the right faraway place, at the right time, and we have the day under control."

With Ma's approval, I pressed the purchase tickets link, as I smiled at my success at still being able to live up to the Boy Scout Motto to "Be Prepared."

The e-mail at the top of the list on Saturday morning was an announcement from the Pesky Proscenium Players advising that the performance for that day was canceled due to illness, which made me feel ill. Rechecking the movie listings, I became even more ill to see that there were no movies playing that were suitable for the boys.

"Grandma Houston, we have a problem," I announced in her ear.

"Now what?" she snapped, in her most endearing manner.

"Cast members are sick. The play is canceled. We are entering rough waters."

My daughter's car pulled up to the front door twenty minutes early, as usual. The two guys popped out of the car, bounded up the front steps, entered the house, removed their shoes, and began to ice skate in their socks over our slippery and shiny wood floors.

"I want a snack," Energy said.

"Me too," Nuclear chimed in.

"But you just had breakfast," I reminded them.

"Yeah, but that was a real long time ago."

"We'll get something to eat at the zoo," I announced.

"I don't want to go to the zoo again. We always go there," Nuclear said.

"This is a special zoo — one you've never been to."

"There's no such thing as special zoo. Seen one, seen 'em all," he observed.

"What kind of special zoo is it?," Energy asked.

"A horse zoo."

"I've never heard of a horse zoo," Energy noted.

"That's why we're going there. It's very exciting."

"What do the horses do at the horse zoo?," Energy asked.

"Oh, they run around and try to catch and pass each other," I said.

"You are not taking my grandsons to a racetrack," Rinnce exclaimed.

"I want to go to the racetrack," both boys screamed, jumping up and down.

Rinnce, Spittella, and our neighbors still have not talked to me since I took the boys to see the thoroughbreds run. The boys, however, keep asking when we're going again.

"As soon as the social workers from the Family Services Agency stop following me," I tell them.

"RESPONSABILLYABEE"

"Grandpa's here," my daughter called out to my two grandsons.

"Which Grandpa?," both boys asked in unison.

"You only have one Grandpa," their Mom replied.

"Yeah, but he flips. Sometimes he's Grandpa and sometimes he's 'Grump-pa,'" came the singular, double response.

"Well, today it's Grump-pa," I said growling, as I picked up Energy and twirled him over my head, slam-dunked him onto the sofa, and tickled him unmercifully.

"When's breakfast?," Nuclear asked.

"Pa will make you English muffins. And Dad, don't let the boys watch television after I leave. You're the one who is always complaining that it makes them brain-dead, decreases their attention span, and stifles their curiosity and analytical skills."

"Do you know how to make English muffins, Pa?," the boys asked in unison.

"Well, I know how to make Chinese muffins, French muffins, Nigerian muffins, Brazilian muffins, and Indonesian muffins, but no, I don't know how to make English muffins."

"Pa, you just stick that muffin over there into the toaster," they both said, speaking as one again.

"Yeah, Pa, you have to take some 'responsabillyabee' to know how to make us English muffins," Energy stated confidently.

"Who's Responsabillyabee?," I asked. "Is he one of your new friends?"

"No Pa," he replied. "It's a thing, not a person."

"What kind of thing?"

"You know, the kind of thing you're supposed to have when you mess up your room, so you can clean it up."

"Oh, that responsabillyabee. There must be two of them like there is two of me."

"Let's play chase us," they pleaded.

"No, it takes too long for my knees to recover," I confessed.

"Well, just be slow and sneaky and trap us then," Nuclear suggested.

"I'm leaving," Mom announced. "Dad, don't forget, Ian's school bus comes at 8:40. Then, no more television for Oren."

"Only four more minutes," I announced to Nuclear who lay on the couch in his pajamas watching the television.

"Okay," he grunted, remaining totally motionless.

"No, Ian. It's not okay. It's 8:36. You only have four minutes to get dressed and catch the bus."

He rose from the sofa like a rocket rising, and in one continuous, choreographed move, he removed his pajamas, pulled up his pants, pulled down his sweater, stepped into his shoes, slipped his arm through his backpack, and ran through the screen in the door, leaving a cut-out in it as if he were a cartoon character.

"This is a good movie you're watching, Energy," I said, as I sat on the couch.

"We have to turn the television off," he reminded me.

"No, it's okay. This is a good movie."

"Mommy will be real mad if she sees us watching television when she gets home."

"No, not if it's a good movie," I replied.

"I thought I told you to turn the television off when I left," Mom screamed when she got home.

I pointed to Energy, and Energy pointed to me, as together we said "He made me do it."

PIECE OF CAKE

It landed on the front porch with a thud. I ran to the door to see what it was, but all I saw was a large box and the back of the UPS truck pulling away. The box and I wrestled with each other like two sumo wrestlers, and I declared myself the victor when I finally put the box down in the corner of the play room and emptied its contents.

"What is it?," Rinnce asked.

"It's not our house, and I didn't order it. Spittella must have ordered another plaything for the boys, since they are so deprived of toys."

"Well, this one looks pretty special," Rinnce remarked.

I picked up the thick instruction pamphlet and began to read the first page.

"Wake up, wake up," Rinnce screamed, as she shook me violently while I slept standing with the instructions in hand.

"What happened?," I mumbled, confused and disoriented.

"You fell asleep — standing — before you even finished the first page of the instruction book."

"Here, you read it and tell me what it says."

"You are so pathetic," she cried, as she took it from me with a look of disdain.

She began to scan the opening page, but her eyes glazed over and closed, accompanied by a whistling snore. "Wake up, wake up," I cried, shaking her to and fro.

"What happened?," she mumbled, confused and disoriented.

"You fell asleep — standing — before your eyes reached the bottom of the first page," I said with delight. "Welcome to 'Club Pathetic.'"

"What the devil are they talking about? This isn't even written in English."

"*Au contraire, ma femme*, but it looks like the King's English to me," I replied with glee.

"Oh, wow, it's here!"

"I turned to see Nuclear cartwheeling toward us."

"What exactly is this 'oh wow' thing?," I asked.

"This is a 'Super Voltage, Wango, Wizzameree, Florellified, Mussgong,'" he said.

"Thats right," I said. "Do you know how it got here?"

"Of course, I ordered it."

"How did you do that?"

"Duh! The same way you order stuff."

"Oh, so you have your Dad's credit card that he can't find?"

"Somewhere."

"Pa can't figure out how to make the Mussgong work," Ma blurted out before I could speak.

"Here, let me show you Pa. It's a piece of cake."

"What kind of cake?"

"Are you being sarcastic, Pa?," he asked.

I looked at him. He looked at me. We both looked at Ma.

"Do you know what sarcastic means?," I asked first, and then Ma asked second.

"Yeah, it's wise-ass talk."

I looked at Ma; Ma looked at me. Neither of us replied.

"It works fine," he announced, as we stood silently watching him bent over and running his fingers over the buttons, knobs, and switches until a motor started, lights blinked, bells rang, and whistles blew.

"What?," he asked, as we stared in wonder.

"Good job," I replied. "I couldn't have done it any better."

"I know, because it was such a piece of chocolate cake," he shot back.

ROOTS AND BRANCHES

Through the blur of failing eyes, I saw a well rooted, solid trunk with a new branch proudly standing amidst the others. And in the low volume of diminished hearing, I listened to the words being said. They came from my grandson, whom I no longer called "Nuclear." His solid trunk of a body rose above the podium behind which he stood. His arms, like long branches, waved in rhythm with the words he spoke.

"Today we celebrate who we are, why we are here, what we have learned, where we are going, what we hope to do, and how we hope to do it when we get there. We all march to the beat of a different drummer, and we all sing and dance to different tunes. But in the end, we all are part of the same song, the title of which is 'Family.' And that is why I have always loved to spend time looking at family photos, whether they were mounted in frames on the wall, filling the pages of albums, or just randomly thrown in a box.

"But even more, I love receiving postcards, especially from my grandparents — who travel a lot. I have saved them all, and I love to read them over and over again. My grandfather has two favorite phrases he likes to say: 'Entertain me,' and 'Send me a postcard.' And, in fact, he sends us postcards from wherever he and my grandmother are. It doesn't have to be in some faraway, exotic land. Sometimes, he sends them from around the corner.

"One of my favorites came from France, when I was very young. It was addressed to my parents. It said: 'Staying at a chateau overlooking a vineyard with grapes named Syrah, Viognier, and Merlot, with colors all around us as bright as a Van Gogh. Looking forward to sharing our stories with you over a few beers and escargot. Tell the boys that escargot is the French word for pizza.

"My favorite photo is of a Schwedler maple standing majestically on a slope overlooking a valley and river below. My mother called it 'the crying tree,' because the ashes of both of my great grandparents were spread under and around it.

"Years ago, my brother and I would mow the lawn on the slope. The lawnmower would always skid on the river side of the tree. Over time, a curved bare mark was carved into the grass.

"I remember the day that my brother and I told my parents that 'the crying tree' was smiling. We showed them the skid mark which was almost half a circumference of a circle around the tree. We said that the tree must be happy that we were all together, and that we should call it 'the smiling tree,' instead of 'the crying tree.'

"That was the first time I really heard the song of my family, and it was then that postcards took on more meaning for me. My mother told me how her grandparents had sent postcards to her, just like my grandparents sent postcards to me. She told me that after her grandparents died, she no longer ran inside to get out of the rain, but instead she would run outside to run in it, hoping that it wouldn't stop. She wanted to feel the raindrops that splashed against her face, because they were now the postcards that she looked forward so much to receiving from them.

"Why we are here, what we have learned, where we are going, what we hope to do, and how we hope to do it when we get there is inextricably tied to the tunes inside all of us and the songs of our families."

As Ian stepped away from the podium and returned to his seat, I remembered one of the physicians who lived in the hootch in Vietnam who would make collages of the family photos his wife kept sending him. At the end of his tour, all four walls of the room in which he bunked were completely covered with family. It was his protective armor.

Novella Nottingham approached me. Her granddaughter Nora was in Ian's class. In contemporary terminology, they hung out together.

"You should be very proud, my good friend, at how Ian turned out. My granddaughter and I will catch up with you at Ian's party at the saloon shortly," she said, with a smile that was one of my best.

GIFT

As Ian and Nora worked the crowd at the saloon, Ian's brother Oren sat at our new player piano with Rinnce. They were lip-synching together to one tune after another to the delight of everyone.

"So much for authenticity," Lyon Couch took great pleasure in noting, while looking exceptionally dapper without his pacifier.

"How's this for authenticity?" I said, as I gave him a hug.

"What am I, chopped liver?," Hoot chimed in.

"Probably more of a pâté," I replied, before giving him his hug.

"Well, I guess that leaves me the odd girl out," Novella observed.

"Join the scrum," I called. "All for one, and one for all."

As the four of us stood off to the side, Ian and Nora came up to us.

"That was one terrific valedictory address you gave young man," Novella told him.

"Thank you Mrs. Nottingham."

"So, kiddo, what are you going to do with that future waiting for you?, Hoot asked."

"Didn't Pa tell you, Uncle Hoot?"

"No, he doesn't tell me anything. He thinks I'm just a pile of pâté."

"I want to be a veterinarian."

"What made you decide on that, dear?," Novella asked.

"It was that story my Pa wrote when I was very young."

"Which story was that?," Lyon asked.

"The one about the dog named Frizbi."

"I thought I'd read everything that your grandfather has ever written," Novella stated, as she looked at me with a look of disapproval. "Can you tell me what the story was about?"

"Oh sure. I can actually tell you the story. I know it by heart."

"Let's sit here in Uncle Hoot's booth," Novella said, as she took Ian's hand. "I'd like to hear it."

FRIZBI

Freddie Forrester, a freckled, seven year old bombshell of energy, with tousled hair and an ear to ear smile which displayed a toothy changing of the guard, stood sadly beside his father watching Dr. Worthington euthanize his dog Zach. He wondered if he would always feel this sad. Dr. Worthington put his hand on Freddie's shoulder as they walked out of the treatment room back into his private office.

"Freddie, I know that this is a very sad time for you, but I need your help. Do you think you could bring yourself to help an old veterinarian like me, even though you're feeling so sad?"

"I don't know," Freddie said. "What do you want me to do?"

"Wait here for just a minute, and I'll show you," Dr. Worthington replied. "I'll be right back."

"What do you think he wants me to do, Dad?," Freddie asked, as he sat on a chair in front of Dr. Worthington's desk, swinging his legs and trying to hold back his tears.

"I don't know, Freddie; we'll just have to wait and see."

The door to the office opened, and Dr. Worthington entered carrying a very small puppy on a blue Frisbee.

"Freddie, I want you to meet Frizbi," Dr. Worthington said. "His mother passed on yesterday, just like Zach. He has no where to go and no one to take care of him. I was hoping that maybe you might agree to adopt Frizbi and to look out for him. I know what a wonderful friend you were to Zach, and Frizbi really needs a good friend right now." He placed the blue Frisbee with Frizbi on Freddie's lap. "Here, you just keep an eye on him while I go help another sick dog. I'll be back soon. You can let me know then."

Freddie looked down at Frizbi on his blue Frisbee. A tear fell from Freddie's eye onto Frizbi's nose. Frizbi wiped it away with his paw while looking up at him. Freddie picked him up, and Frizbi began to lick away Freddie's tears. Freddie was very confident that he'd be able to help Dr. Worthington. That night, Frizbi slept on his blue Frisbee beside Freddie's bed.

Frizbi and his blue Frisbee were inseparable. After sleeping on it, he would drag it about and chew on it. When it was time for Freddie to go to bed, Frizbi would carry his blue Frisbee to his bedside and go to sleep on it. As Frizbi grew, his affection for his blue Frisbee did not wane. Although he could no longer sleep on it, he slept with it.

Freddie and Frizbi played together frequently, and it was Frizbi's Frisbee that fueled their love for each other. Freddie and Frizbi would play tug-of-war with the Frisbee, as Frizbi growled with delight and tried to not let go. Whenever Freddie would break Frizbi's clench on the Frisbee, he would toss it gently away, and Frizbi would run to it, pick it up in his mouth, and return to Freddie to resume the tug-of-war.

As Frizbi got older and bigger, and as Freddie got bigger and stronger, the gentle toss of the Frisbee became a classic Frisbee throw: a high gliding spin that sent the Frisbee farther and farther away from Frizbi, who would run faster and faster, and jump higher and higher, to catch it. Now, when Frizbi would bring it back to Freddie, they would not have a tug-of-war, but just repeat the Frisbee launch and Frizbi's race to the horizon and jump to the sun.

Freddie and Frizbi became famous. Frizbi won blue ribbons, red ribbons, green, and gold ribbons, as well as plaques and statues of jumping dogs. Then, on a rainy Saturday morning when Freddie awoke, he found Frizbi lying motionless by his bed with the scratched, scuffed, chipped, and chewed blue Frisbee under his paw. One of Freddie's tears dropped onto Frizbi's nose, but Frizbi didn't wipe it away or look up at him, like he had done many years before. Freddie lay down beside Frizbi and draped his arm over his body. He lay with him for a long time. Later, he dug a grave in back of the house. He made a cross on which he attached the blue Frisbee. On it he wrote: "The horizon is far and the sun is high, but my Frizbi will guide me to them both," which he did. Freddie Forrester is now Dr. Frederic

Forrester, D.V.M., practicing Veterinary Medicine, as a specialist for dogs.

Recently, a young girl of seven stood silently beside her mother as Dr. Forrester helped the girl's dog find eternal peace. She wondered if she would always feel this sad. Dr. Forrester put his hand on the girl's shoulder as they walked out of the treatment room back into his private office.

"Jennifer, I know that this is a very sad time for you, but I need your help. Do you think that you could bring yourself to help an old veterinarian like me, even though you're feeling so sad."

"I don't know," Jennifer said. "What do you want me to do?"

"Wait here for just a minute, and I'll show you," Dr. Forrester replied. "I'll be right back."

"What do you think he wants me to do, Mom?," Jennifer asked, as she sat on a chair in front of Dr. Forrester's desk, swinging her legs and trying to hold back her tears.

"I don't know, Jennifer, we'll just have to wait and see."

The door to the office opened, and Dr. Forrester entered carrying a very small puppy on a pink Frisbee.

"Jennifer, I want you to meet Frizbi. Her mother passed on yesterday, just like your dog Elsie. She has nowhere to go and no one to take care of her. I was hoping that you might agree to adopt Frizbi and to look out for her. I know what a wonderful friend you were to Elsie, and Frizbi really needs a good friend right now." He placed the pink Frisbee with Frizbi on Jennifer's lap. "Here, you just keep an eye on her while I go help another sick dog. I'll be back soon. You can let me know then."

PAID IN FULL

"You know, Spit," Novella said in her special way with her head cocked and her left eyebrow raised, "I think you may have just checkmated me."

"Come on, Novella, we aren't even playing chess."

"Come on yourself, Salvatore Spittell Toon, D.M.D. We're always playing chess. And every breath you take and word you say is a chess move on the chessboard of life."

"Now, now Novella, even if that were true, I haven't said anything. Ian just finished telling you a story, not me."

"But it was your words which he spoke."

"So, he checkmated you, not me."

"No, no, no. How many years have we been doubling and redoubling our bet about your place mat stories and poems?"

"More than I'd like to admit. If we were betting chocolate ice cream sodas like I did with my roommate in college, the exponent which would determine the number I owed you would be longer than infinity."

"Exactly!"

"And your point is?"

"I concede. You've just won your infinite number of double or nothing bets. You don't owe me a thing. Your story is somewhat coherent, as well as somewhat autobiographically styled. I relieve you of your obligation to get it published somewhere, which relieves me from facing the fate of having my face on the dart board near the bar. Do what you wish with what you have woven."

"I don't know whether to be happy or sad, Novella. You know that bets like we've had are at the heart and soul of my being."

"No, I finally believe that they are not. They are just one of the many ways you play your game of not letting anyone inside. But that simple, little story shows me that special je ne sais quoi that I wanted to see."

"And all along, I thought you were so hard to please."

"Well, your softer side becomes you. Your family becomes you. You're nicely in tune with the family Toon. Relax big guy. Smell the roses."

"Gee, I thought that's what I was doing."

"No, stemming from what I've seen and heard for so long, you've been confusing the petals with the thorns."

COKE BOTTLE GLASSES

"How's that?," the optometrist
asked, as he slipped my new
glasses on.
"Spectacular," I replied, despite
being worried that I would be
making a spectacle of myself
wearing these new coke bottle
spectacles.
But as I walked out of his door and
into the world, which had previously
been a blur to me, the curtain rose, the
music started, and I took my seat to
enjoy the spectacle of life, for which I must
admit that I was delighted to have a ticket.

BLUR

The glasses that were on my nose
were no longer there in repose,
but hiding where no one knows
and adding to my daily woes.
Agitated and blindly shaken,
I retraced the steps that I had taken,
only to not see them any place
because they weren't on my face
to provide vision very clear
through the blur far and near.
High and low from ceiling to floor,
I looked and looked and then once more.
Then my wife joined in the search
and looked on every shelf and perch.
Soon she turned and looked at me,
and lo and behold what did I see
but my glasses on her face,
which she had put on in place
of her own, which were not around,
so she just used what she found.

FOREBODING

The joy of Novella's concession didn't last long. A strange feeling was insidiously beginning to metastasize throughout my soul. The comfort of the metronomic beat of the saloon's daily ritual did not seem as strong. I missed our steady customers, who were like family, when they were called to new places. The new customers were always welcome and fun to get to know, but it was never the same as it was in the beginning. The change that makes everything the same fooled with our senses and feelings. The rhythm continued, but the beat, unheard and unfelt, began to slip away, ever so silently, in such small increments that you were unaware that it was happening. The intangible chemistry of all interaction began to give off invisible cues of dilution and diminution. Ennui, such a poetic word, but drug-like in feeling, flowed gently through the heart and soul of daily activity. Life was the same, but it also was not. Sometimes it seemed better, but not better than the beginning.

The next next that was certain to come seemed to be off schedule. In the distance, which didn't seem as faraway as before, there was a blank grayness, a fog that blurred what you knew was there. Inexplicably, the Prosecco bubbles seemed more lethargic. The thought of the fragility in the air applied a pressure of unease. I was feeling like I was swimming upstream in saliva even though I had gotten out of the mouth and into the world. My reflection in the mirror looked like the poster child for the "Beware of What You Wish for Campaign." The foreboding feeling would not let go. I wondered what would happen and when.

The very next day, Hoot asked me to join him for lunch in "Hellman's Booth." I was delighted, as I hadn't seen much of him lately.

"So, where have you been of late, Hoot?" I asked as we clicked our glasses of Prosecco. "The saloon is never the same when you're away."

"A spark ignited some stuff from the past. I had to put my fireman's hat on."

"Everything okay?"

"Everything is too much to hope for. Hopefully, enough is okay."

"Well, that's pretty enigmatic."

"Life is a mystery, *n'est-ce pas?*," he said more than just philosophically, but with what I thought was a touch of melancholy. I mentioned to Rinnce how I thought something might not be right with Hoot.

"Give the poor guy a break, Spit," she countered. "For as long as we've known him, he's always been upbeat, solid, and steady. In a certain way, it's reassuring to know that even he can have a down day."

"No, I sensed that this was bigger and deeper than just a down day. He didn't want to talk about it."

"None of this is surprising, Spit. You and I have discussed, more than once that, as wonderful as Hoot is, and as much as we love him, there seems to be one page in his book that he doesn't want us, or anyone, to read."

Rinnce was right, which only intensified my concern for my friend. I knew that he didn't want me to pry, so I just hoped that, in time, more than enough would be fine.

VALLEY OF ASHES

I was awakened in the middle of the night by sirens. The brightness of fire darkened everything. I walked toward the saloon, but it was not there. It was a pile of ashes. Looking out over the wasteland, I remembered reading F. Scott Fitzgerald's description of a cinder dump in *The Great Gatsby*. He called it the "valley of ashes." I watched the ashes being lifted into the air by the swirling wind. They were like flakes of snow which were black, not white; and rising, not falling. At that moment, I knew that the blackness which had descended upon us would be blown away, leaving something reinvented in its place. But first there would have to be an investigation.

All Rinnce and I wanted to do was to never look back, to combine our insurance settlement with the assets received from liquidating everything else we owned, and to purchase a residence on a large ship that cruised the world.

It took some time, but after the investigation of the fire had been completed, that's what we did. The investigation determined that the saloon had succumbed to arson and that Hoot, although not deemed to be the arsonist, was in some way integral to the events, and it was on Hoot whom the investigation ultimately focused.

Rinnce and I spent many hours being interviewed by the authorities. We told them everything we knew, or thought we knew, about our friend, but apparently that page in his book, from which he wanted no one to read, was the key to the case. In the end, Hoot was gone. His fate was unknown, as were the contents of his private page.

We waved from the ship's deck to Spittella, Brian-Brian, Ian and Oren. And from the darkest recesses of the oral cavity, and through the doors of our former saloon, we moved on to the next next: traveling around the world.

But the "valley of ashes" still haunted us. As time passed, the whereabouts of Hoot were still unknown. After a few years, his memory, while still present, settled somewhat quietly, deep in a retired section of each of our minds.

TIME ON MY HANDS

On a steaming hot afternoon
of risotto thick air, I sat on
on a park bench with time on
my hands.
I uncapped my hands from
around a clock and stared
at my ticking palms.
The deep sweep of time had
worn away skin and drawn
serpentine lines in the sand.
Rotating my arms to bring my
knuckles atop, I saw the bumps
in the road over which I had
stumbled, callously callusing
my view of all.
Blue highway veins ran by
the finger forked turns I
had wrongly made or missed,
while handshakes never offered,
and others betrayed, haunted me.
Life had tipped its hand on
the hands into which I peered,
fingering me and nailing down
a case that didn't need to be made.
I had made my own case: the
one that was handed to me.

CAMUU CAMUU

As was our routine, we went to the ship's piano bar after dinner. Only a few scattered tables were occupied. We each ordered a glass of Prosecco and concentrated on the torch song singer who called herself Fyre, and whom we were seeing for the first time. Although many years had passed, and although her appearance had changed, I still recognized her as the woman named Camuu Camuu who had gotten Hoot into a colossal mess. I was sure that she recognized me, as well.

I traveled one of those serpentine pathways in my mind to go back several years in search of the memory I had of meeting Camuu Camuu. I remembered sitting with Hoot in "Hellman's Booth" when she had approached.

"My name is Camuu Camuu" she murmured.

"As in Albert?," he joked.

"As in Albare, with a silent *t*, and as in Camus with no *s* and two *u*'s," she stated.

She told him that she wanted him to help her commit the perfect crime: the murder of her abusive husband. Offended, but intrigued, Hoot heard her out. She made a compelling case for what she wanted to do.

"I think you might be confused about the role of a private investigator, in general, and also specifically as it applies to me." he suggested. "You see, I'm really a very sensitive guy as my client base has been mostly performing artists: Broadway, cabaret, and lay-away. You must know that I couldn't possibly get involved in such an act."

"Well, at least buy me dinner, then," she said, wiping away a tear.

Hoot didn't have to tell me that on the Hellman zero to ten scale of drop dead gorgeous, Camuu Camuu had scored an eleven. So, I took the cue and excused myself.

The next day her husband was found dead and the story was all over the papers. It's the only time I can remember ever having seen Hoot sweat.

"Hoot, why do you let your zero to ten scale of drop dead gorgeous trump logic and put you in compromising situations, so close to the wrong side of the law?" I asked him. I've never forgotten his response.

"Spit, when you're a private investigator, you're always on the edge. Sometimes, your toenails are over the edge, even if you don't want them to be. You learn to live with it and to hope that the good Lord judges you in the full context of your intentions and actions. Reality sucks. That's why I love life at the saloon. It takes the bad taste out of my mouth.

"I was torn betwixt and between, Spit. She was playing me as well as Yo-Yo Ma plays his cello, except that his music soothes me, and hers was keeping me on edge. Although I was mesmerized by her, I was in an invisible and silent meltdown of panic about her request to help her kill her husband. I was caught in her spell, so, after dinner, when she offered to buy me 'un digestif' at the bar, because 'it was the least she could do,' I blindly followed her. Ask your bartender, Schottzy, and he'll confirm that everyone was taken by her, including him. One drink led to another, and she only said good-bye to her adoring fans as the bar closed."

At her trial for the murder of her husband, the chief witnesses for the defense were Hoot, Schottzy, and several patrons who testified that Camuu Camuu was with them at the saloon from 5 P.M. until 2 A.M. Although the prosecution was able to prove motive, they couldn't prove means or opportunity. Despite her request to Hoot, her alibi was rock solid. With the facts of her husband's abuse, her compelling performance in court, and the best legal team money could buy, the jury conjured up enough reasonable doubt to acquit. Hoot didn't know how she did it, but he did know that she had done it perfectly.

I made my trip back from Memory Lane just in time to hear Camuu Camuu finish her last song and take her bows. Our eyes locked in contact, and after what seemed a long time, she walked toward Rinnce and me. She was still extraordinarily beautiful.

"Good evening Dr. and Mrs. Toon. The world is a much smaller place than most people realize, n'est-ce pas?"

We invited her to join us in our suite, where I opened a bottle of Armagnac, filled our glasses, raised mine, and said "To Hoot."

"To Hoot," Rinnce and Camuu Camuu repeated.

"I was sorry to learn about the fire at the saloon," Camuu Camuu said.

"I guess it was just the next next at that moment in time. Apparently our reunion is the next next of this moment."

"Yes, I believe so," she said, as her eyes watered. "Hoot loved to use that phrase."

"We haven't heard from Hoot since the fire. The authorities think that he was somehow integral to it, although they don't believe he did it. Have you heard from him at all?"

She put her head in her hands and sobbed harder than I had ever heard anyone do before. Rinnce and I sat in silence, not exactly sure what she might say. It was several minutes before she came up for air, wiped her eyes, and regained her composure.

"There is so much that you don't know," she continued. "I feel so badly that you don't. I don't know where to begin."

Rinnce and I looked at each other. We saw our anxiety in each other's eyes. We both knew that the blank page in the book of Hoot was about to be filled.

"I'm sure that I don't have to tell you that Hoot had a secret. Because I knew it, I was able to use him, as I did, to kill my husband. He didn't kill him; he never knew how he was killed; and he never asked me to tell him how I arranged it. But he knew that I had made him an accessory by having dinner and late night drinks with him at the saloon."

"Which he did because you threatened to reveal his secret if he didn't," I interjected.

"Yes."

"But his secret was revealed to certain parties by his appearance in court, which put him in harm's way."

"Yes."

"And the fire at the saloon was to save him, as well as Rinnce and me," I surmised out loud.

"You and Rinnce, most certainly. Himself? I don't think he's confident that he can save himself, and I don't think he gives a hoot if if he can't. I assume that you would like to hear my tale."

"You betcha," Rinnce and I said together. Then we sat back and listened to her for a long time.

SECRETS

Camuu Camuu started the story right where my memory had ended: when I left Hoot's booth. She told us that the first thing he said to her was that he hoped she understood that there was no way he could break the law for a client. She told him that she understood perfectly, but that she wasn't asking him to help because of his profession, but rather because of his identity.

"My identity?," he repeated.

"You know perfectly well what I mean," she noted firmly.

"But I would like to know perfectly well what you purport to know," he asked with equal firmness.

"How could I bluff about something like this?," she said.

"Well, who is you husband? Perhaps that will help put this in perspective for me."

"Marco."

"Marco?"

"Yes."

"Does he have a last name?"

"Mortia."

"I see," Hoot said softly, as he began to sweat, something he never wanted anyone to see him do. And until that moment, no one ever had, because no one was better under pressure than Hoot Hellman, Private Investigator, no matter how far back into a corner the pressure pushed him. But Camuu Camuu had used her trump card.

"I assume, then, that you will help me," she pressed.

"And, if I don't?"

"Then the world will know that you were not born Harvey Hellman. Wouldn't that be a hoot?"

Hoot knew that it wouldn't be a hoot, but rather a catastrophe. You see, Marco Mortia was Hoot's brother. You could say that's a euphemism for "it's a long and complicated story," but here's the oxymoronic, sanitized down and dirty.

Hoot Hellman was a whoops baby, born ten years after Marco, who until Hoot's arrival on the scene was an only child. Hoot's father died shortly after his birth, by what is known in the circles in which he traveled as a "rub out," which was carried out because of family wrath incurred by one of his indiscretions. Hoot's mother relied heavily on her husband's brothers while raising her two boys. When Hoot was eight, Marco was taking his first step up the ladder on which he would climb to the heights of criminal power. When Hoot's mother died, he was eleven, and he was taken in by one of his uncles. Hoot hated the shadow that darkened his family name. By the time he was sixteen, he knew that the only way he could get free from being a Mortia was to disappear and to reinvent himself. And that's what he did.

One day Hoot did not return home from school. He had saved enough money from odd jobs for his breakaway, and he made it across the country to San Francisco on his thumb and freight cars. An obituary about a Harvey Hellman caught his eye. Thinking it had a safe sound to it, he decided to take the name as his. Soon enough, he realized that he needed more than safe. He needed a flourish that fit his crafted persona of individualism and strength. He came up with Hoot because "people sort of stayed clear of owls." As a matter of necessity, he lived below the radar screen, surviving on a mixture of street smarts, luck, a few good samaritans, some petty theft, and forged papers. He was not particularly proud of some of the things he did, but he never looked back, because he would only have gotten hit by what was in front of him.

It turns out; however, that as Hoot kept looking and moving forward, he walked right into the arms of his Uncle Sam, who barely reviewed his forged papers and automatically stamped them with the military's approval. All Hoot had said were the magic words: "I want to enlist," and he had made some recruiter very happy.

Two tours of duty through thick Vietnamese jungles burned his family history in an incendiary blaze of napalm. He returned to San Francisco as the kind of guy people would rather not mess with, but one whom they would rely on to do their dirty work. It didn't take him long to see that all he had to do was to call himself a private eye, and he would assume enough legitimacy to make his way through life. Hoot discovered that success bred success, and pretty soon he was able to call his own shots and to create his own niche. He evolved into his Broadway, cabaret, lay-away persona, even though he wasn't under the shadow of the George Washington Bridge, but rather the one spanning out from the Golden Gate.

Life was good, except for one thing. His wife Linh, whom he had met in 'Nam, worked hard to bring back to the States, and with whom he had enjoyed a blissful marriage, was murdered. The police never solved the case. But he had his suspicions, although he couldn't prove them.

Despite the fact that Camuu Camuu scared the hell out of Hoot, he was still attracted to her. It had been a long time since a woman had that effect on him: a real long time, dating back to 'Nam. And since Linh's murder, no other woman had cast a spell on him the way Camuu Camuu had.

"Look Camuu Camuu, you've really blindsided me," he commented as calmly as he could, although the prospect of having his true identity waved to the world held him in panic's clutch. He knew he was in extremely, dangerous waters. "Exactly why do you want to kill your husband?," he asked.

"I'm trapped in a situation about which I had no prior awareness. Of course, it's my own fault for being naïve and for allowing myself to be swept off my feet by Marco. Once I married him, 'family' had a much bigger meaning than anything I had ever envisioned. There was, and there is, no way out for me unless Marco is out of the picture. Then, like you, I need to disappear and reinvent myself."

"You're starting way later than I did, and I doubt that you can disappear."

"There are people who can make me disappear right before your eyes."

"I'm not following you," he noted, although he knew where she was going.

"Plastic surgery and a new identity," she replied.

When Camuu Camuu walked out of the courthouse, she never looked back, and Hoot had no idea where she went, where she was, what she was doing, and whether she had changed her looks.

That all changed about a year later. He was finally doing some of that traveling he had always talked about, but had never done. He was in Paris, walking one *arrondissement* at a time, when he walked into a café on a side street near the *Gare du Nord*. It was a hole in the wall which was not up to his expectations, but he was tired and hungry, so he decided to stay. The food was good, as it was pretty much everywhere in Paris, and the wine went down easily.

The longer he stayed, the more tired he got, which meant he stayed even longer, because he was too tired to leave. A woman began to play a piano in the corner and sing intermittently. As he was getting up to leave, she began to play "I left my heart in San Francisco." He walked toward the exit, not paying attention to the music. But then he realized the *chanteuse* was singing the song in English. He stopped, turned around, and then stepped aside to listen. She had that "she looks like someone else you knew" face. But Hoot always thought someone looked like someone else. He left before she finished the song. A block or two down the street, he stopped. He realized that it wasn't her appearance but rather her voice which had been tugging at his memory. Wondering if he was stretching his assessment a bit too much, Hoot still decided to return to the restaurant. He asked for a seat close to the piano.

Although he knew that his staring was making her uncomfortable, he couldn't help himself. She could have been Camuu Camuu, but then again, she could have been anybody. Her hair was black, not blonde. Her nose wasn't the same as he remembered, nor were her eyes the same color. Even her teeth had a different look. Although he assumed that Camuu Camuu would have changed her appearance, he still knew that he was over-analyzing way too much. Someone requested a song, which she sang.

"*S'il vous plait, un autre chanson en anglais?*," he asked when she finished the song.

She looked at him for what seemed a long time, and then she said "*Non, pas ce soir*."

"What is your name?," he asked, as he got up to leave.

"Alberta," she replied.

"As in Albert?," he asked.

"No, Albert has a silent *t*. Alberta has a hard *t* sound," she explained, with what he was sure was a twinkle in her eye.

"You look familiar," Hoot pressed. "Where else have you performed where I might have seen you?"

"I believe you confuse a familiarity with my sound, not my appearance. I confess to modeling my musical interpretations after others."

"Would you share un digestif with a single, lonely, American male after your show?"

"Perhaps. I'm not sure. Are you a gambling man?"

"I think my invitation has proven that I am."

"I play for another hour. There is a nice bar across the street called *Vin Ordinaire*. No bet is a sure thing, but if you are willing to take a chance, I may follow-up on this evening's chance meeting. If I am not there by midnight, then I will not be joining you."

Hoot sat at a comfortable table in a corner at Vin Ordinaire savoring a glass of *Château d'Yquem* and wondering whether she would show up. Each time the front door opened, he looked with anticipation. Time was running out. He looked at his watch and decided to wait for a few more minutes. Finally, he got up from his table and walked toward the door with a heavy heart. It swung open just before he reached it. They stood face to face. Her eyes were filled with tears. She turned and ran away.

Hoot didn't travel again after he watched Camuu Camuu run off into the Paris night. Part of him knew that he was waiting for her to walk through a door to him someday. Another part of him knew that she, like Linh, was lost forever. And all of him wondered why he couldn't find the answer to either loss.

SNOWFLAKE

Our friendship was a snowflake,
germinated from water vapor,
forged in the cold hearth of a cloud,
and hammered on an anvil of hope.
Our eyes were like frosted windows,
through which we marveled at the
delicate lattice of water and ice which
seemed so indestructible.
But the weight of a mere particle of
dust weighed heavily on the
crystalline form causing cracks,
breakage, and melting, which left
only a tear.

WHO SAID THAT?

Rinnce had a liking for a quiz show called *Who Said That*? She was probably the show's most loyal viewer, as well as its most knowledgeable. I finally succumbed to her pleadings to watch the show with her. And for months, floating on the sea, we watched together the contestants duke it out over famous quotations.

A new round of four contestants began their competition: two men and two women. The last contestant standing was the winner. The emcee began.

"Who said 'I can't wait until tomorrow, 'cause I get better- looking every day?'" Both women and one man knew it was Joe Namath.

"Who said 'Marriage is a great institution, but I'm not ready for an institution yet?'" One man and one woman knew that it was Mae West.

"Who said 'Bigamy is having one wife too many. Monogamy is the same?'" The woman knew that it was Oscar Wilde.

We decided to be members of her fan club, because we liked her name: Gutta Percha Packer. We thought it was a hoot, as gutta percha is a dental filling material which is packed into root canals. She told the emcee that her father had been an endodontist, a dental specialist for root canals, and that he had always loved the sound of the words gutta percha. She said all her friends just called her G.P. We followed her loyally as she won twelve straight rounds, which qualified her for the championship round.

"Who said 'Man invented language to satisfy his deep need to complain?'" The sole male contestant got it wrong, but G.P. and the other two women knew it was Lily Tomlin.

"Who said 'Humor is just another defense against the universe?'" Not only did GP and the other two women know that it was Mel Brooks, but all three got the next eight questions correct also.

We were glued to our sets the following week. After another four questions, one woman faltered. Now it was down to only two: G.P. and her opponent named Mary.

"Okay, the first one to miss a question is out, and the lone lady standing is our champion and will win one million dollars," the emcee, who irritated the hell out of me, announced.

"Who said 'God writes a lot of comedy, but the trouble is, he's stuck with so many bad actors who don't know how to play funny?'" Both G.P. and Mary got it wrong. The correct answer was Garrison Keillor

After six questions, they were still tied, and we had to wait another week. And at week's end, we were there and ready to root G.P. on. She and Mary were still tied halfway through the show.

"Who said that he realized that he was God when he was praying, because he was talking to himself ?"

Mary paused for a seemingly long time and then said "Spit Toon." I almost fell off my chair. But then G.P. agreed. This time I did make it to the floor. Rinnce knew that the correct answer was Peter O'Toole. They remained tied. I concentrated on every detail I could think of about each woman. There was nothing that gave me any hint whatsoever that I knew either one. And yet, they had both incorrectly attributed that quote to me. How could that be? I got back in my chair, took a deep breath, and waited for the battle to resume.

"Who said 'We wait. We are bored. No, don't protest, we are bored to death. There's no denying it... A diversion comes along and what do we do? We let it go to waste... In an instant all will vanish and we'll be alone once more, in the midst of nothingness!'"

G.P. answered Eugene Ionesco; Mary answered Spit Toon. I was beside myself. I knew something wasn't right. I thought back to which woman said Spit Toon the first time my name was given. I couldn't see any helpful pattern developing.

"No, I'm sorry; you're both wrong. The answer is Vladimir in Samuel Becket's *Waiting for Godot*. You remain tied," the irritating emcee squealed in delight. "I believe that we are out of time, but next week might be it. Good luck Contestant Number One."

"Thank you. See you next week."

"Good luck Contestant Number Two."

"Thank you. Until the next next."

"Rincce, what is going on here?," I said from the highest point of the orbit I was now in.

"Apparently, you have two fans," she surmised.

"But who are they?"

"Probably some tourists who passed through the saloon and bought a box of the complete place mat collection."

"No, there's more to it than that," I claimed.

It was a long week. When the favorite hour of our favorite evening arrived, Rincce and I were leaning forward, staring hard and white knuckled.

"Who said that the truth is that everyone is bored and devotes themselves to cultivating habits?"

Mary answered "Jean Paul Sartre." G.P. replied "Spit Toon."

They were both wrong. The correct answer was Albert Camus. Still there was no consistency as to whom would utter my name, first or second. Moreover, I could not comprehend why I was being mentioned at all.

"This will be the final question. If you are both right, or if you are both wrong, you will split the one million dollar prize," the emcee announced.

"Who said 'Until the next next?'"

Mary's answer was "My opponent G.P., last week while saying good-bye." G.P.'s answer was "Spit Toon."

"You are both right," the emcee screamed, as he jumped up and down like he needed to rush to the lavatory. "We'll be right back after our break for an interview with our two amazing contestants."

We waited anxiously through all the commercials, and then we we both honed in on each woman.

"Don't laugh," I said to Rinnce, "but listen real carefully to G.P.'s voice."

"I don't hear anything special," she said.

"Doesn't it sound more like a guy's voice?"

"Not especially. Maybe she's got laryngitis."

"Maybe," I replied, unconvinced and with my eyes and ears on high alert for anything that would address my visceral suspicion.

"Rinnce, look at G.P. again. Open and close your eyes a few times. Turn your head away from the screen and then turn it back. On certain angles, in certain lighting, there's a certain familiarity to her face."

"She doesn't look like anyone I know."

"I think she looks like Hoot," I said, fearing her reaction.

"Lots of people of either gender look like someone else, even of an opposite gender," she noted, much more calmly than I expected. "You of all people understand spitting images," she then added.

"It's Hoot; I'm positive."

"Nonsense. If that's him, he's had a sex change."

"Exactly! Even with voice surgery and/or conscious voice control, there could still be something of the original voice present, especially if the person is fatigued and lets his or her guard down," I explained. "Whoa baby, I bet he's in witness protection. And the burning question is why, although it is most likely connected to the burning of the saloon. He probably turned in his family. But why would he draw attention to himself, or herself, by using my name. The last thing he or she would want to do is to indicate a connection to me."

"Maybe he's hoping we are watching. Maybe he wants us to know he's okay. Maybe he hates his life and doesn't care if his cover is exposed."

"This qualifies as a 'wowwer.'"

"Maybe I should send that in as a quotation question for the program," Rinnce suggested. "You know Spit, we can go through hoops trying to sort it all out, but in the end it won't change anything. At least we know he's alive, even if we don't know all the details. Although what we know is more than we were bargaining for."

"Do you think Camuu Camuu knows?," I wondered aloud.

"Let's not ask her. Let's leave her alone. She's got enough stuff on her plate."

"I bet Lyon's going to choke on his pacifier when he hears this," I said, still shaking my head in wonder.

"You know Spit, I've got to hand it to Hoot. He looks a lot better in a dress than you did at that conference I dragged you to, where the girls dressed you in drag."

The two of us walked out to the deck and stood at the railing looking out at the sea.

"I think we've done enough latitudinal and longitudinal full circles of the earth," I said. "It's time for the next next."

MAILBOX

A first class memory, well
stamped in my mind, seemed
to arrive overnight expressly
to envelope me in nostalgia
for my childhood home.
Although I was boxed in a
mailbag lifestyle of insufficient
postage, I made it a priority to
try to find a way to travel by
air to where I was born.
I finally was able to deliver on
the special promise I had made
to myself, so I posted an e-mail
to those whom should know, and
I began my journey home.
As I turned my rental car into the
driveway of the home to which I
had returned, a doorless, dented,
and rusted mailbox, hanging
precariously to a wobbly, decaying
wooden post, waved weakly to me
in the breeze.
The river, which ran through the valley
below, seemed as unchanged to me as
the memories to which I clung, but as I
turned toward the house, I caught my
reflection in a shattered glass window.
All I saw was a doorless, dented, and
rusted mailbox, hanging precariously to
a wobbly, decaying wooden post.

PINE CONE MEMORIES

Brittle pine cones
crunch underfoot,
while others hang
tenuously behind
stringed curtains
of green needles,
waiting for what
will befall them.
These are my
memories, fallen
and fragile, awaiting
the grim black
funnel of wind
which will suck
them away forever.
Until that moment, I
reap my memories from
the sound of the crunch
underfoot, the whistle
of the wind, and the
creaking of the swaying
limbs.

Eric Kobb Miller

FULL CIRCLE

I closed my eyes and the mailbox fell from view. As I turned away from the shattered window, I saw the tree under which my parents' ashes were spread. I saw my father spreading the ashes of my mother. Then I saw myself, thirteen years later, spreading his ashes, trying to duplicate the pattern he had made. I remembered the nuclear energy like explosion of an intensely deep, pink sunset when his last ash had fallen to complete his reunion with my mother.

The voices of Nuclear and Energy were calling out: "Look, 'the crying tree' is smiling. It must be happy that we are all together."

The sky gave off a greenish glow, tinted with a faintness of red. Happy children danced on the sky to the music of a band called Northern Lights and the voice of a singer named Aurora Borealis. I wondered if they knew any tunes from the family Toon.

I remained under the tree until the sun had fully set. A full, snow white moon took over the sky. Then, jackal like clouds attacked the vanilla, gelato scoop of a moon, first circling and then scampering across to smother its light. With sharpened hooves they knocked off white gelato chips which fell into the dark emptiness to begin the long descent to the soiled earth below. I watched them become transformed into white gelato flakes which gently tantalized outstretched tongues of frolicking children and slow strolling lovers.

Under that tree, I slept on the ashen ground until I awoke the following morning to see contrails in the sky. Although they were ice crystals formed by planes flying through freezing cold air, they blanketed me in warmth. The white inked sky spoke words of mythic Greek and Roman gods which mapped undiscovered thoughts.

Time passed, and I waited in a state of wonder: wishing, wanting, and listening for a whisper in the wind. When it came, it was inaudible. I felt withdrawn, wistful, walled off, whittled and weathered, as if I were floating on a whiff of whiskey and a splash of waterfall.

Two deep snow powder clouds emerged from beyond the horizon, one behind the other. Pushing off on their skis, they slalomed between ethereal moguls before schussing with avalanche speed the rest of the way. As they reached the base of the run, just above the river, they sparred with their poles over whom would be mizzen and whom we be main, but the decision was rigged by a gust from the wind. Thrust onto undulating white crested waves, they sailed on the river's surface in a sea of passion toward the rising sun. I imagined them watching the sun's descent at the end of the day, as they wondered if it would be clear sailing tomorrow.

"I am saffron rice raindrops from chorizo clouds in a paella sky," I heard Rinnce say from faraway.

"And I am snowflake confetti from a skyscraper top," I silently thought to myself.

"I ran to you through sunflower fields," I heard her say softly.

"And I skied to you on powdery snow," I whispered back to her.

"We met on a raft of Beaujolais corks and sailed together on rivers of wine," lyrically wafted toward me.

"The far distant shore awaits our reunion, where we will rest on a bed of sunflower petals covered with a blanket of snow," I murmured.

An image of the family Toon appeared on the canvas sky. All the faces were spitting images of one another. The jigsaw puzzle pieces from so long ago were now all locked in place, except mine. I was the next piece waiting to be fit into place. A man at a piano played a Spit tune. I didn't know if he was lip-synching, or if it was a player piano at which he sat. He looked, and the music sounded, authentic. I saw and heard a machine gun spit bullets of my whole life in a fast forward blur of images and incoherent jibberish. It was my life, but anyone could have claimed it as one's own, because in the end we are all spitting out images of whom we think we are or want to be. We are spitting images of each other.

SPITTING IMAGES

I had an image of
myself, the one of
whom I thought I was.
But it spun on a wheeel
in a perpetual blur in
which I saw myself in
others, and others within
me.
And what I imagined to
be unique, broke into
pieces of a shattered
mirror, which I then tried
to piece back together into
something new.
But like time which spits
out change in which the
new mirrors the old, my
reassembled mirror reflected
spitting images of me.

Acknowledgments

The sad clown on the cover was painted by my father, Harvey Miller, when I was a sophomore in college. It has hung on a wall wherever I have lived, ever since.

Many of the linked place mats of sad songs and funny tales in Spit Toon's Saloon were first published separately in online and/or print publications. In this book; however, they have been used in entirety, in part, combined, and/or with some editing of names, titles, and text. It is with much gratitude that I acknowledge these publications.

Short Humour
The Storyteller
Foundling Review
Bartleby Snopes
Writers' Bloc (Rutgers)
Calliope Nerve
Word Catalyst
Stories that Lift
Shoots and Vines
Troubadour 21
Poetry Friends
Flutter Poetry Journal
Mad Swirl
Callused Hands
No Teeth Poetry
tinfoildresses
Poets Against War (Canada)
A Handful of Stones
Oak Bend Review
Cynic Online Magazine
Bolts of Silk

Eric Kobb Miller is a retired dentist
who has laid down his drill for a quill.
Call him Spit.

Breinigsville, PA USA
17 September 2010

245602BV00001B/9/P

9 781595 943842